Other books by Greg Hoffman

The Art of World Team Tennis

Tennis Love: A Parent's Guide to the Sport
by Billie Jean King and Greg Hoffman; Illustrated
by Charles M. Schulz

Mixed Doubles
by Billie Jean King & Fred Stolle with Greg Hoffman

A Hallelujah Jamboree
The Sister Mary Mummy Stories

A HALLELUJAH JAMBOREE
The Sister Mary Mummy Stories

Greg Hoffman

Illustrated by Frank Ansley

Jorgensen Publishing Company/Los Angeles

To everyone who was there . . . and survived

"After all, any given moment has its value; it can be questioned in the light of afterwards, but the moment remains."

F. Scott Fitzgerald
The Crack-Up

Just one thing
That I've gotta say...
I need a miracle
Every day.

Grateful Dead
I Need A Miracle

Design: Lynne Robinson
Type: Frank's Type/Mountain View, CA
Printing: Balzer-Shopes/San Francisco, CA

Contents

Acknowledgments

Thanks to:

Rosalie Muller Wright, who published the first Sister Mary Mummy Story;

Annette Thompson, who found the perfect illustrator;

Babe Balzer, who laughed louder and longer than anyone;

Cheryl McCall and Larry King, who helped keep the good Sister alive;

Margaret Roach, Doug Latimer, Judy Scheuch, and Sue Hoover, who coaxed her out of the convent after a brief retirement;

Jim Jorgensen and Jim Santy, who were extremely supportive;

Tim and Judi DeWolf, Jef Nimmo, Virginia Powell McIlmoil, Nancy Ditz, and Eileen Sebanc, who offered friendship, encouragement and positive feedback;

and Christine Hoffman, who patiently listened to the stories and suggested I write them anyway.

Author's Note

The first thing most people noticed about Sister Mary Mummy was this: her size. It was said that every once in a while, when the atmospheric conditions were exactly right, her shoulders would ice up like the wings of a DC-3 over the Himalayas and she would have to walk all hunched over until the ice melted.

The second thing most people noticed about Sister Mary Mummy was this: her eyes. Most of the time they were soft and blue with a mischievous conjunctival twinkle, but when she became aroused—a not infrequent occurrence—those placid pools of peace and tranquility were instantly transformed into steel-gray weapons of intimidation. It was said that when this happened her glare could stop a charging water buffalo dead in its tracks and turn it into two tons of quivering, cowering flesh.

Well, maybe the water buffalo bit *is* a little far-fetched, but only because such creatures were rather scarce around Our Lady of the Gulag parish in the late '50s.

Ah yes, Our Lady of the Gulag, the infamous home base and stomping grounds of Attila the Nun, a.k.a. Sister Mary Mummy.

According to popular legend, her tenure (i.e., reign of terror) in the parish's dreary halls of academe began sometime during the early stages of The Hundred Years' War. Legend also insists that she was exhibiting her own *ex cathedra* infallibility long before the first Vatican Council officially proclaimed that Popes are invested with that same attribute.

Though benevolence was by no means foreign to her character, Sister Mary Mummy could be, as she proved on more than one occasion, a ruthless, marble-hearted dictator in the classroom. There is, for instance, the persistent, but unconfirmed tale that she once maliciously flunked an entire class on a mere whim, destroying several dozen lives in the process. It is widely believed Rome gave her a special commendation for that little maneuver.

Naturally Sister Mary Mummy was fully aware of these and the thousands of other rumors that surrounded her. Rather than attempting to set the record straight, however, she gleefully cultivated each and every one of them. To add to her potent mystique, it was even rumored that the good Sister herself was the source of most of the rumors. Of course that particular rumor was started by Sister Mary Mummy.

But amid all the rumors and myths, amid all the exaggerations, half-truths and fables that swirled like so many autumn leaves through the corridors and classrooms of Our Lady of the Gulag year after year for as long as anyone could remember, one incontrovertible fact stands out: Sister Mary Mummy did, in fact, exist.

I should know. After all, I spent nine months in her custody. Nine excruciatingly long and unpleasant months. Trust me.

Greg Hoffman
Palo Alto, California
June 1980

A Hallelujah Jamboree
The Sister Mary Mummy Stories

I

THE FIRST DAY...

FTER A SOLID WEEK of spewing forth violent thunderstorms that were brief in duration but strung together tighter than an expensive strand of pearls, the morning sky finally displayed the sun against a cloudless, blue background.

It was, Dudley Mack decided without really knowing why, a bad omen.

Groaning loudly, Dudley rolled over in his rumpled bed and closed his eyes against the brightness. Then, just as he was on the verge of once again doing one of the few things he was good at—falling asleep—the significance of his vague meteorological observation penetrated the thick cobwebs that enveloped—some would say, formed—his brain.

Wide awake now, he stared at the ceiling and ruefully acknowledged the fact that the first day of school had finally arrived. This displeased him enormously because his hatred of the educational process was positively legendary. Judging by his equally legendary lack of even minimal academic success, the educational process wasn't all that fond of him, either. They were, however, stuck with each other once again. Beginning today.

And so Dudley Mack, the Don Corleone of Our Lady of the Gulag, unleashed a truly inspiring litany of obscenities and pulled the covers over his head on the morning of the first day of school.

❧

A few blocks away, Marty Shea greeted the first day of school the same way he greeted every other day that came his way: calmly and serenely. He was able to do this for the simple reason that practically everything, school included, came easily for him. Although he shared, and at times even surpassed Dudley Mack's renowned lackadaisical attitude towards studying, Marty somehow managed to breeze through class while his unfortunate colleague blundered, collecting bad grades and trouble the way dedicated philatelists collect stamps.

Marty was of course well aware of the fact that he was one of the chosen few, one of those fortunate individuals who are blessed with the enviable ability to effortlessly navigate life's swirling and often treacherous currents, accomplishing much with pathetically little effort, but he wisely pretended not to notice his favored status. Because of this, he was both liked and admired by his peers. Infinitely more importantly, however, he was both liked and admired by himself, although he quite properly shunned public displays of this affection.

As might be expected, Marty was also determinedly even-tempered. In fact it was often said of him that even in the most trying situations, he usually remained as unruffled as the hem of Sister Mary Mummy's habit.

On the morning of the first day of school, therefore, Marty was somewhat dismayed to find his silky smooth disposition severely dented by the realization that he would have to see Jimmy Sullivan every day for the next several months. Although he made every possible effort to be tolerant of Sullivan, he couldn't quite pull it off. The little creep annoyed Marty tremendously, just as he annoyed every other person who wasn't a legitimate candidate for sainthood.

"You know what Sullivan is?" Dudley Mack had said a few days earlier. "He's the fingernail on everybody's blackboard."

Marty Shea smiled as he recalled Dudley's words. Then his thoughts of Sullivan evaporated as quickly as they'd come, and he resumed his strictly-observed regimen of calisthenics, most of which were of his own invention.

～

At that exact moment, the object of Dudley Mack's unkind, but thoroughly accurate description was on his knees pawing through a heroic pile of junk that had accumulated on the floor of his bedroom closet.

C'mon, you guys," whined Sullivan in his peculiar, certifiably annoying, nasal voice, "I know you're in here. You might as well give up and come out right now, 'cuz I'm gonna find you sooner or later."

Jimmy Sullivan was addressing a pair of sneakers he had misplaced.

～

While Dudley Mack was agonizing under the covers; while Marty Shea was working out; and while Jimmy Sullivan was pitifully pleading with his missing footwear; Mary Margaret Delicate was proudly gazing at her crisply-uniformed reflection in a full-length mirror.

"Perfect," she said softly. "Absolutely perfect."

A series of clumsy pirouettes convinced her that the shapeless blue pinafore, garishly emblazoned with an embroidered "G" over the left breast, adequately camouflaged any physical attributes she might have developed over the summer, which, of course, she hadn't developed at all.

Though Mary Margaret wasn't particularly thrilled with the design of the unattractive garment, she was deeply grateful for it. That's because all of Our Lady of the Gulag's female students, including Suzy Fondell, were required to wear them. Besides having silky, blonde hair that moved even when she wasn't, Suzy Fondell was, at 14, better endowed than Harvard. Mary Margaret hated her almost as much as she hated Dudley Mack, but for entirely different reasons. Her dislike of Suzy was firmly rooted in female jealousy; her dislike of Dudley was firmly rooted in her long-held conviction that he was a subhuman whose sole reason for being was to make her own life miserable.

Reluctantly turning her back on the mirror, Mary Margaret focused her attention on the composition she had written the first day of summer vacation. As always, she was momentarily impressed by the elaborate, flowing penmanship that graced the lines of her notebook, and she congratulated herself on yet another job well done. She was especially proud of the dainty butterflies that floated ethereally above each "i" in the manuscript. Mary Margaret had spent countless hours experimenting with elegant hearts and the more artistic (and time-consuming) butterflies, before deciding the latter should replace the slightly *passé* circles she had been using for some five years.

"Ain't it bad enough that she thinks she's got a halo over her head," Dudley Mack had grumbled when Mary Margaret's circle fetish had surfaced in the third grade, "does she have to spread 'em all over her lousy homework, too?"

The composition was entitled, "What I Did Last Summer," and she had written it because of her firm belief that a paper on that topic would be assigned on the first day of school. Needless to say, Mary Margaret was usually better prepared than a troop of overly-conscientious Boy Scouts.

Mentally giving herself an "A" for content, and a similar mark for neatness of presentation, she dropped the neat pack of lies into her shiny new book bag and headed downstairs.

Unfortunately, her perfectly-postured descent was abruptly terminated when she caught her foot on the edge of the third step and fell down the remaining six. The accident transported Mary Margaret to the brink of hysteria because, although she was unhurt, her immaculate brown and white saddle shoes were badly scuffed. In her personal catalog of Things To Be Avoided At All Costs, one scuff was worth at least a dozen wrinkles, and a wrinkle on Mary Margaret was rarer than a Quaker hit man.

So on the morning of the first day of school, Mary Margaret Delicate's nutritionally-balanced breakfast was flavored by her tears of frustration.

～

Shapeless uniform notwithstanding, Suzy Fondell's mere presence in a classroom was almost as disruptive as a fusillade of Dudley Mack spitballs or one of Mary Margaret Delicate's not infrequent crying jags.

By some strange quirk of nature, Suzy had successfully negotiated puberty sometime during the fourth grade and since then she had devoted every moment of her existence and every ounce of her considerable energy towards becoming, as she so charmingly put it, "... the very best cheerleader in the entire United States and maybe even Texas." She was awfully good, too, no doubt about it. She was so good, in fact, that Dudley Mack, Our Lady of the Gulag's premier athlete, was constantly threatening to quit the football team so he could sit in the stands and watch her perform.

"Either that," Dudley was fond of saying with a practiced, adolescent leer, "or Coach'd better design some plays that'll get her into the huddle."

Suzy was excited about the first day of school because

it meant that she could once again practice her cheers before a large and appreciative crowd of male students during the lunch recess. That an equal number of female students would view her performances with a mixture of envy and disgust bothered her not at all.

"I only hope I don't misspell any cheer this year," she said to herself as she sat on the floor between her pompons and tried to remember how to tie her shoelaces.

The little blonde with the leather pipes and the remote control hair was still haunted by an incident that had occured during the homecoming game the previous year. As usual, the Our Lady of the Gulag "Crimson Tide" were behind by six or seven touchdowns at halftime, but Suzy's spirit had remained embarrassingly undiminished. As the teams trotted onto the field to begin the second half, she began to lead the sparse crowd in a cheer.

"Give me a 'V'," she yelled into her blue and white "Crimson Tide" megaphone.

"V," shouted the crowd except for one smart aleck who yelled, "Five!"

"Give me an 'I'," yelled Suzy.

"I," screamed the crowd in an attempt to keep warm.

"Give me a...uh...uh..." Suzy faltered for a moment, but her recovery was swift and sure. "...a 'K'."

The crowd, quite obviously puzzled by the strange request, responded with a feeble, "K?"

"Give me a 'T'," yelled an undaunted Suzy.

There was no response forthcoming, and the rumble emanating from the stands seriously upset her rhythm, but Suzy bravely pressed on.

"Give me an 'O'," she bellowed with all her might.
Silence.

"Give me an 'R'." Her voice was beginning to crack.
Dead silence.

"Give me a 'Y'," Suzy whispered. "*Please.*"

By this time, both teams, the coaches, and the referees

were staring at the little girl who had managed to silence an entire crowd. Suzy's hair was the only thing in the stadium that was still moving.

Finally, after a long, painful pause, her anguished wail split the still night air.

"Give me a *VIKTORY!*"

Suzy Fondell was saddled with the body of a sex goddess and the intelligence of a Boston fern.

⁓

Though some teachers dread the first day of school almost as much as some students do, Sister Mary Mummy definitely wasn't a member of that club. On the contrary, she had, throughout her long and illustrious career as a shaper of fertile young minds, habitually looked forward to the start of each new academic session with eagerness. If it is true, as Alban Goodier wrote in *The School of Love,* that "the enthusiastic, to those who are not, are always something of a trial," a lot of folks were in for a very rough time. Especially one Dudley L. Mack.

Hours before the aforementioned Mr. Mack (Sister Mary Mummy addressed every male student that fate and circumstance had delivered or ever would deliver into her orbit as "Mister") and his fellow students were scheduled to turn themselves in, the enthusiastic nun was scurrying around her eighth-grade classroom on the third floor, making sure everything was in order. She had already arranged the 30 scarred desks into five meticu-lously-aligned rows, and she had washed the three large blackboards not once, but twice. Finally, after assuring herself that further sweeping, dusting and straightening would amount to gross domestic overkill, Sister Mary Mummy began to study the class list Sister Superior, Our Lady of the Gulag's feisty principal, had given her the previous evening.

With the possible exception of a transfer student or two, everybody on that list was painfully aware of the woman who was to be their instructor. But while Sister

Mary Mummy was familiar with most of the names, there were several she didn't recognize and this bothered her a great deal. Like Mary Margaret Delicate, she was a firm believer in being prepared. After all, she reasoned, it was 30 against one in the classroom.

"Better make that 29 against two," Sister Mary Mummy muttered, noticing that Delicate, Mary Margaret was listed right above Fondell, Suzanne. In midsummer, she had received a certified letter which gushingly announced that Delicate, Mary Margaret planned to become a nun at the earliest opportunity.

Grimacing as she recalled the swarm of butterflies that had infested Mary Margaret's blatantly transparent attempt to gain early favor, Sister Mary Mummy put the class list aside and settled her bulky frame into her structurally-reinforced swivel chair. For the fifth or sixth time this morning, she rummaged through the vault-like drawers of her massive oak desk. This check, like each of the previous ones, confirmed their emptiness, but she was convinced that they would be overflowing with confiscated contraband long before the month was out. In fact the coming year promised to be her best ever because Dudley Mack's name was on the class list, and Dudley, as she knew only too well, was a walking hock shop.

Finally satisfied that all was in readiness, Sister Mary Mummy leaned back, put her feet up and began to watch the institutional clock that hung on the wall above the door. Its hands were moving alright, but they weren't moving nearly fast enough for her.

&

And me?

What was I doing on this glorious, September morning so long ago?

Oh, nothing much. I was just engaged in my usual first-day-of-school ritual which basically consisted of hanging out in the bathroom and throwing up every 30 seconds or so.   &

II

THE DRIBBLING NUN AND OTHER MENACES

HE NUN ESCORTING ME to the principal's office was mad as hell, but the intensity of her anger paled beside the sheer terror that gripped me. I felt as though I was floating, which, in fact, I was. This was primarily due to the fact that the nun was propelling me forward with the generous handful of my shirt collar she had gathered into her massive right fist. I touched down about every ten feet or so.

Sister Mary Mummy, my none-too-gentle escort, was a very tall woman of indeterminate years who, in her long black habit, somewhat resembled a vertical limousine. A gigantic rosary encircled her substantial waist and rumor had it that the rosary's chain had been salvaged from a wrecked Harley-Davidson. That particular rumor was, to the best of my knowledge, never confirmed.

I can confirm this though: No matter how long I live, I will never—repeat, *never*—forget the sound that infernal rosary made. As Sister Mary Mummy and I marched and floated through the empty corridors of Our Lady of the Gulag that winter afternoon, its distinctive *clickety-clack* was greatly amplified by the tiled walls, lending a macabre cadence to our, I mean my, death march.

Our noisy journey to the principal's office was the direct result of the momentary, but quite complete lapse of sanity I had suffered a few moments earlier. I had, in full view of the entire eighth grade class, written and solved—albeit incorrectly—an arithmetic problem on the front of Sister Mary Mummy's habit. To make matters even worse, it was a complicated word problem. Something about two trains as I recall. Anyway, to this day I don't know what sinister force motivated me to perform such an obviously senseless, not to mention suicidal act. Perhaps I possessed some sort of adolescent death wish or something. I am, however, firmly convinced that my twisted action was not caused by anything as romantic as an unquenchable thirst for adventure, because since birth I have thirsted for nothing more than anonymity. Unfortunately, a logical explanation for my behavior, unlike the chalk on Sister Mary Mummy's habit, did not exist.

When I proudly underlined my incorrect solution with a dramatic flourish, two of my horrified classmates actually fainted. But Sister Mary Mummy didn't move a muscle. She just stood there like the Rock of Gibraltar and fixed me with a look that clearly said, "I am not thrilled with what you have done."

"Sorry, S'ter," I managed to stammer. "I thought you were the blackboard."

Three more of my fellow students hit the deck and I began to feel a bit lightheaded and dizzy myself.

Sister Mary Mummy totally ignored my flimsy attempt at a defense, grabbed the back of my shirt collar, and quickly carried me from the silent classroom.

While I was dangling from the end of her right arm like

some kind of human charm bracelet, the irate nun tried to brush the chalk off the front of her habit with her free hand. Suddenly, and quite perversely, I realized that was probably the only task for which she had neglected to appoint a monitor. I decided not to volunteer though. Somehow the timing seemed to be, ah, shall we say, inappropriate.

To reach our ultimate destination, it was necessary for us to pass through Our Lady of the Gulag's ancient gymnasium. As we burst through the worn wooden gym doors, I happened to notice that someone had left a basketball lying on the warped floor. This was a gross violation of the Sports Equipment Code, and I was on the verge of pointing it out to Sister Mary Mummy in the hopes that it would divert her from her present mission, but she'd already seen it.

She stopped brushing her habit and, without breaking stride or releasing her grip on me, she reached down and palmed the basketball. I was properly awed, but Sister Mary Mummy appeared to be oblivious to the fact that she had just performed a miracle of sorts. I mean the average person just doesn't go around casually palming basketballs.

Then she did something even more unbelievable. Without so much as a glance at the basket, she sunk a 35-foot hook shot. With her left hand. I immediately forgot my predicament.

"Excuse me, S'ter," I said, "Could you show me that shot again?"

Without a word, she dropped me like the proverbial hot potato and I ran to retrieve the ball. She took it from me, dribbled a few times and then leaped at least 36 inches straight up. A perfect jumper... *Swish.*

A twisting layup from the right side... *Swish.*

A double-pump layup from the left side... *Swish.*

A right-handed hook from the top of the key... *Swish.*

10 out of 10 free throws, five with her left hand and five

with her right.

The incredible display of shooting prowess ended a few minutes later when Sister Mary Mummy *drop-kicked* the ball through the rim from half court.

I couldn't believe it. She was without a doubt the greatest basketball player I had ever seen, maybe even the greatest who ever lived. I tried to communicate that fact to my friends later, but I was spectacularly unsuccessful. It was inconceivable to them that any female, and especially a nun, could play basketball at all, much less with the degree of proficiency I was describing. They remained unconvinced until several months later when Sister Mary Mummy surprisingly accepted our polite, though very insincere invitation to participate in our daily lunchtime softball game.

"I'm pitchin'," said Dudley Mack, exhausting approximately 75 percent of his working vocabulary.

Dudley, the best athlete and worst student in the history of Our Lady of the Gulag, was a huge, overdeveloped kid who had been blessed with exceptional athletic ability and an exceptionally abrasive personality. Nobody particularly liked him, but we were all too scared to show it. Consequently, he was the most popular member of the class.

"OK, gang, who's going to pitch?" asked Jimmy Sullivan, an energetic, sparkplug of a guy. We all hated Sullivan almost as much as we feared Dudley.

"How about ol' Dud doin' the pitchin'?" said Marty Shea sarcastically.

"Good idea," said Sullivan. "Hey, Dudley, why don't you pitch?"

"I'm pitchin'," said Dudley Mack.

As usual, I was assigned to play catcher and it was in that capacity that I called a pre-game conference with Dudley on the pitcher's mound.

"I'm gonna bean her," he said menacingly.

"No, Dudley. Please don't do that," I pleaded. "Pitch

her easy. Let her hit the ball. *Please.*"

"I'm gonna bean her," Dudley repeated.

I gave up and trotted to my position behind the batter. Sister Mary Mummy was impatiently tapping home plate with the business end of her bat.

"Ready, S'ter?" Dudley shouted.

"I'm ready, Mr. Mack," she replied. "Let's see what kind of stuff you've got."

The ball left Dudley's hand and, as he promised, it sailed directly towards Sister Mary Mummy's head. I promptly froze, but Sister Mary Mummy gracefully removed her considerable bulk from the path of the ball. Then, at the last possible second, she reached out with her bat as if to block the pitch. Snapping her wrists viciously at the moment of impact, she smashed a drive that was still rising as it passed over the leftfielder's head.

Though obviously shaken by the four-bagger, Dudley Mack struck out the next three batters on nine pitches. His teammates were shouting excitedly as they ran in from the field.

"Nobody hits Dudley like that!"

"She barely even swung!"

"Whatta shot!"

"Sister Mary Babe Ruth!"

"She was just lucky," spat out Dudley Mack. "Just plain lucky."

Sister Mary Mummy, who was on the mound for the opposition, declined the traditional warm-up tosses and motioned for the first hitter. Sullivan, our leadoff man, went down swinging as usual. "Fat" Chance then chased a high outside pitch and popped out to the shortstop. Dudley was up next and we all knew it was all over for Sister Mary Mummy. Dudley was a truly prodigious batsman who cursed anything less than a triple. Although quite a few home runs had been hit over the chain link fence that enclosed our makeshift diamond, he was the only person ever to put one onto the roof of the lumber yard across the street. In fact he did it almost every time he stepped into the batter's box.

"C'mon, Dud, baby," Sullivan screeched, "hit that sucker outta here. Park it in the next county."

Most of Dudley's teammates, myself included, secretly hoped he would strike out like we mere mortals had been known to do on occasion. That was highly improbable though. Dudley never struck out, and that's never with a capital 'N'.

Sister Mary Mummy waited until Dudley stopped fidgeting in the box before commencing her wind-up. The gleaming softball emerged from the folds of her swirling habit and split the plate waist-high as Dudley swung mightily and missed completely.

"That's OK, Dud," Sullivan screamed. "You'll get the next one."

Sister Mary Mummy's second offering materialized from the billowing black cloth and it, too, bisected the plate. Again Dudley swung from the heels, and again he missed badly.

Almost as incredible as Dudley's consecutive whiffs was the fact that Sullivan, to the relief of all present, suddenly ran out of encouraging words. The only sound on the field was the ominous *clickety-clack* of Sister Mary Mummy's rosary beads as she wound up for her third delivery.

The first two pitches had been fastballs, but this one fairly danced and floated towards the plate. It wasn't spinning at all. Sister Mary Mummy had served up a perfect knuckleball that caught the anxious Dudley Mack completely off guard. He swung awkwardly, then stumbled and fell face down across the plate well before the ball gently settled into the pocket of the catcher's waiting mitt. Dudley lay there in the dirt for a very long time before he got up and shuffled to the mound.

Two innings later Sister Mary Mummy inadvertently, though mercifully, ended the game with a towering blast that carried *over* the lumberyard roof. By the time we finally located the ball, the lunch recess was over and we had to return to the classroom where Dudley Mack immediately continued his eventually successful attempt to avoid obtaining a legitimate education.

But he did learn one thing that day. Like everyone else who participated in that infamous softball game, Dudley Mack discovered that not only does the Lord move in mysterious ways, so does Sister Mary Mummy's curve ball.   ✎

III

CLEATS
IN THE CONVENT

E STARED at the approaching nun with fear and amazement. Since the football practice field was located nearly four blocks from the school her appearance obviously meant that one of us was in big, deep trouble. Recognizing this, several of my teammates donned their helmets in subconscious gestures of self-defense. Meanwhile, well-rehearsed looks of innocence automatically plastered themselves on the faces of those who chose to remain unmasked. I hurriedly conducted a hasty review of my recent activities, but I failed to come up with anything that would cause Sister Mary Mummy to leave the confines of the convent, track me down at football practice and take me into custody.

As she ambled across the end zone, Sister Mary Mummy paused to give the goal post an affectionate pat. A large manila envelope was clutched in her right hand.

Marty Shea was the first to speak. "Oh God," he moaned, "she found it." He was referring to the barely

20 SISTER MARY MUMMY

legible remnants of a girlie magazine he kept hidden in
the deepest recesses of his cluttered desk...in a large
manila envelope.

"Plead insanity," someone suggested. "After all, you
know what they say about..."

"Shut up," hissed Marty Shea.

"Good afternoon, boys," said Sister Mary Mummy,
who was quite a bit larger than our entire starting back-
field. The more observant players noticed that she was
wearing a pair of high-topped black tennies instead of
the clunky leather shoes she usually wore on duty, and
that her rosary, a primitive, though effective Early Warning Device, was missing. A large silver whistle dangled
from the chain around her neck.

"Good afternoon, S'ter," we chorused, blending our
voices in a manner that would have made the Lennon
Sisters envious.

"Boys, or maybe I should call you men," she said,
pausing while the team shared a nervous pre-pubescent
laugh, "I have an announcement to make. Some of you
won't be very happy with what I'm about to say. In fact,
most, if not all of you will be disappointed to some
degree."

Thoughts of mass suspension raced through my mind.

"I," continued Sister Mary Mummy, "am your new
football coach."

That particular bombshell was met by silence, bowed
heads—helmeted and bare—and a whole lot of self-con-
scious dirt-kicking. Only Marty Shea seemed not to mind
the prospect of being coached by a nun, but then his attention was almost entirely focused on the manila envelope. The rest of us, true to Sister Mary Mummy's
prediction, would have preferred a less ominous reason
for her presence on the football field that afternoon.

We had managed to develop into a fairly incompetent
team under the guidance of the recently departed Coach
Howell, and we had even come to love his complete lack

of football knowledge. If we somehow managed to run two offensive plays in a row we considered it a "drive", while holding the opposition to less than 50 points was an outstanding defensive effort worthy of celebration. Now, saddled with a nun for a coach, we were sure to be laughed, as well as run, out of the league.

Finally, Marty Shea summoned up the courage to speak. "Whatcha got in the envelope there, S'ter?"

"Plays," replied Sister Mary Mummy. "When I was asked by Monsignor Munchkin to fill in until a replacement for Coach Howell is found, I decided to work out a few simple, offensive plays."

"But we already got some plays," protested Dudley Mack, our first-string quarterback and one of the few players on the team blessed with the ability to hold onto the football for more than three or four seconds at a time.

"We already *have* some plays," corrected Sister Mary Mummy. "I'm well aware of that, Mr. Mack. However, I think these plays, unlike the old ones, will be effective."

She then began to distribute mimeographed pages covered with neat, little O's and X's. Our previous playbook had consisted of crudely drawn sketches executed in loose dirt by Coach Howell's stubby forefinger, and I was attempting to cope with the sudden sophistication being thrust upon us when I was singled out as the recipient of Sister Mary Mummy's first insult. Insults are considered to be an art form by most coaches, and they are dispensed at regular intervals.

"Where did you get that helmet, Hoffman? Did you cut it off the back of a box of Wheaties?"

"Actually," I replied lamely, "it was a box of Cheerios." The helmet in question was a red and green antique my uncle had given me several years before. It was made of pliable leather that was far more decorative than protective.

I decided to quit the team.

But Sister Mary Mummy had another announcement.

"Men," she said solemnly, "I want to be treated exactly like you treated Coach Howell. Just forget that you spend every day in my classroom."

"Sure thing, Sister," I thought to myself. "And while I'm at it I'll forget the Pope's Catholic."

Before we had a chance to disperse for calisthenics, little Jimmy Sullivan, our feisty left halfback, positioned himself next to our new coach. We all valued Sullivan's presence on the team because he provided us with an overwhelming sense of togetherness. In other words, we all hated his guts.

"Can I have your attention, guys?" Sullivan yelled. About half the team began doing calisthenics and the other half wandered off in groups of twos and threes to discuss the merits of Sister Mary Mummy's plays. Sullivan, as usual, was oblivious to the lack of attention he commanded. "Fine," he said. "Now as you guys know, we have a mighty big game coming up with St. Francis. If we work hard, and more importantly, if we work *together*, we can show those turkeys how this game of football was meant to be played. Sure, we've had our problems in the past, but now we have a new coach, new plays and new determination. From now on a touchdown won't just be something the other team does every few minutes."

Sister Mary Mummy appeared to be a bit agitated, but nothing was going to stop Sullivan. He was really rolling.

"So come on, guys," he screamed, "let's go out there and win one for the Sister!"

"Thank you, Sullivan," said Sister Mary Mummy.

"A quitter never wins and a winner never quits!"

"Thank you, Sullivan," said Sister Mary Mummy.

"Defeat is worse than death because you have to live with defeat!"

"Thank you, Sullivan," said Sister Mary Mummy.

"Winning isn't everything, it's the *only* thing. Remember, guys, *God is on our side!*"

"Shut up, Sullivan," said Sister Mary Mummy, and he did.

"Those slogans are very impressive," she continued, "but I don't think they'll even come close to winning a football game. Also, I really think God will be fairly objective about our game with St. Francis."

Sullivan muttered something about St. Francis being undefeated and went off to practice being a left halfback.

Our workout that day was, unlike any previous one we had experienced, an exercise in efficiency. Sister Mary Mummy halted our usual tendency to run several offensive plays at the same time, and she gently pointed out that not everyone should go deep on pass patterns.

"Actually, someone should try to hang back and block for the quarterback," she said. "Preferably some of you linemen."

She also outlawed our most successful offensive weapon: the forward fumble. We had spent a lot of time perfecting that particular maneuver and were quite upset at having it removed from our arsenal.

Surprisingly, by the end of the week we were actually playing as a team, an experience I found to be enjoyable, and I decided not to quit the squad. Of course, my decision was slightly influenced by Sister Mary Mummy's excellent judgment in promoting me to first string. I was unable to hold onto Dudley Mack's bullet-like passes, but I was the only one stupid enough to try.

"Like this," Coach Mummy said after I dropped yet another one. She sprinted downfield about ten yards, then cut sharply to her left as Dudley rifled the ball. Though he failed to lead her properly, she just reached back and hauled it in one-handed and without breaking stride.

"Right," I mumbled.

Dudley, in an obvious attempt to impress the coach, suddenly began calling signals in fractions.

"¼...½...⁵⁄₁₆...HIKE," he would say.

"Whole numbers will do, Mr. Mack," said Sister Mary Mummy.

Dudley then began showing up at practice with fistfuls of highly complex plays, carefully diagrammed. Sister Mary Mummy glanced at the plays and suggested that if he put half as much time and effort into diagramming sentences he just might find himself in possession of a passing grade in English. "Besides," she said, "I doubt whether the Baltimore Colts could execute any of these plays in less than five minutes." If Dudley was disappointed he didn't show it, although I thought I detected a slight increase in the velocity of his passes.

～

Finally, Game Day was upon us and Sister Mary Mummy waited in the bus as we put on our uniforms in the church basement.

"She's not a bad coach after all," someone said.

"Yeah," another agreed, "she's like a regular person."

"Too bad she can't get married and have kids and stuff," ventured "Fat" Chance. "She'd make a great mother."

His remarks were greeted by a chorus of assenting comments and we soon found ourselves involved in a discussion of the relative merits of celibacy.

"I think it's some kinda permanent penance," suggested Marty Shea. "You know, three Hail Marys, three Our Fathers and forget S-E-X."

"I'm pretty sure it's voluntary," chimed in Sullivan, "but there's some sort of secret compensation."

"You're both wrong," said Dudley Mack. "It's hereditary."

Later, during the ride to the game, Sister Mary Mummy announced her retirement from coaching. A permanent coach, a non-cleric male, had been found. We said we wanted her to be our coach.

"Thank you, men," she said, "but I'm sure you'll do very well with a proper coach. I just want you to know that I'm very proud of you. All of you."

We were proud of her, too, but we didn't say it. I think she knew it though. At least I hope she did.

And I would like to be able to say we worked ourselves into an inspirational frenzy and knocked off undefeated St. Francis, but I won't because we didn't.

The final score was 63–zip.   ◞

IV

·

SOULS ON ICE

ISERABLE WEATHER and Monday morning ... normally the double-barrelled bleakness of that combination would have been more than enough to touch off a widespread outbreak of severe depression among the inmates at Our Lady of the Gulag. On that miserable Monday morning, however, our collective mood was actually quite buoyant because it signalled the glorious end of our month-long assault on the surrounding community, an event otherwise known as The Our Lady of the Gulag Paper Drive.

For four long weeks we had been scouring the streets and relentlessly badgering our neighbors with but a single goal in mind: the acquisition of as many old newspapers as we could get our grubby little hands on. But acquiring the loot was only the beginning. Once the papers were in our possession, we spent hours tying them into haphazard bundles which we then lugged to the correctional facility that was cleverly disguised as an institution of lower learning. The nun in charge of each class had the unenviable task of weighing each precious bundle, recording that weight next to the luggee's name and, finally, adding the day's accumulation to the class total.

Sister Mary Mummy registered the contributions of the eighth-grade scavengers, and she did it with quiet authority and efficiency. As a veteran of countless paper drives her expertise in such matters was beyond question. That, however, certainly didn't prevent us from questioning it. Upon submitting a pile of paper to the weigh-in, each of us would assume both an attitude and a posture of studied nonchalance intended to hide our acute fear that she would short us even a fraction of an ounce. Of course our pathetic efforts failed miserably and we ended up looking exactly as if we were afraid she would short us a fraction of an ounce. Only Mary Margaret Delicate professed complete faith in Sister Mary Mummy's calculations.

"Aren't you going to hover over me and watch every move I make while trying to pretend you couldn't care less, Miss Delicate," said Sister Mary Mummy one morning, "like the rest of these clowns?"

"Oh, no, Sister," gushed Mary Margaret, "not me. *I* trust you completely."

"Of course she trusts her," muttered Marty Shea. "That explains why she brings in a bill of lading with each delivery."

The bills of lading—neatly typed in triplicate, accurate to the third decimal place, and duly notarized—typified Mary Margaret Delicate's approach not only to the paper drive, but to life itself. No detail, in her estimation, was too small to be ignored. And nothing, absolutely nothing she did escaped clarification, classification, or categorization. If it couldn't be cubbyholed, she wanted no part of it. But even without the bills of lading, Mary Margaret managed to add new dimensions to the art of newsprint offerings merely by remaining slavishly true to her personal motto, "Neatness and Completeness: The Crossroads of Perfection."

While the rest of us mere mortals bound our stacks of paper with twine or string that, more often than not, failed to survive the trip from home to the weigh-in, Mary Margaret's compact bundles were held together with satin ribbons expertly tied into large, picturesque bows.

"Unfair!" screamed Jimmy Sullivan the first time Mary Margaret presented one of these ostentatious creations to Sister Mary Mummy. "The crummy bow alone must weigh three pounds."

Sister Mary Mummy promptly overruled Sullivan's objection by fixing him with a stare that would have frozen a charging water buffalo dead in its tracks.

"But on the other hand," crooned Sullivan, "it *is* awfully attractive."

We of course had not the slightest idea as to what the eventual fate of the eight piles of newspaper in the alleyway between the school building and the convent might be, nor did we much care. We were also quite unconcerned with the prize of an outing and a bronze plaque that would be awarded to the class contributing the most poundage. That one had gone to the eighth grade every year and, judging by the size of our pile in the alley, we were in no danger of breaking precedent.

Being greedy souls, however, each of us was most interested in the individual grand prize of $50 in cold, hard cash. That was an outrageous fortune in our eyes, and one that most of us equated with long-term financial solvency.

"If I get the 50 bucks, the first thing I'm gonna do is get me a new set of wheels," said Sullivan one morning during our daily trek to school. He was dragging two large bundles of paper along the sidewalk.

"Good idea," said the bundle-less Marty Shea. "I noticed the ones on your trike are getting kinda rusty."

"No," sputtered Sullivan, "I mean—"

"Well, *I'm* either going to invest in real estate or give it to the starving children in China," interrupted Mary Margaret, shifting a beautifully wrapped bundle of yellowing paper from one arm to the other. As usual she was wearing a vinyl rain slicker and a pair of heavy-duty work gloves in a wholly successful attempt to protect both her uniform and her flesh from becoming smudged with newsprint. She was deathly afraid of smudges and stains, and we all clearly remembered the horrible day several years earlier when her pen leaked and she got a tiny spot of ink on her sleeve. When she finally noticed the stain, Mary Margaret shattered the silence of the classroom with a piercing scream that practically gave everyone a coronary. Even Sister Mary Mummy went pale at the sound. And although the hysterical student pleaded for the Last Rites, she had to settle for sedation and three days in bed.

"How about you, Marty?" asked Mary Margaret.

"What will you do with the money if you win?"

"Oh, I don't know," replied Marty Shea. "Maybe I'll just blow the whole wad on having the printer's ink surgically removed from my hands." Upon saying this, he thrust a handful of blackened fingers in front of Mary Margaret's face, causing her to turn away in disgust.

"I meant a *car*," whined Sullivan. "A big, shiny Merc with—"

This time it was Dudley Mack who interrupted him. "You're all crazy," said Dudley. "You guys ain't gonna win the money. I am."

"*You*?" shrieked Sullivan. "How? You haven't even brought in one lousy scrap of paper yet and the drive ends in less than a week." He began to laugh his distinctive and singularly irritating laugh. "Did you guys hear that? Ol' Dud here thinks he's gonna win the money. What a laugh."

"And what makes you so sure I'm not?" said Dudley

Mack, advancing toward Sullivan menacingly.

"Nothing, Dud," said Sullivan, wide-eyeing Dudley's massive right fist, "absolutely nothing. Matter of fact, I think you have an excellent chance, a really excellent chance. After all, it's never over until it ends."

"Since he's so positive he's going to win, ask him what he plans to do with the money," said Mary Margaret Delicate to no one in particular. For many years she had refused to communicate directly with Dudley Mack.

"Sooo ... what are you going to do with the money, Dud?" asked Sullivan, continuing his anxious attempt to preserve his facial features.

"I'm gonna save it," announced Dudley. "You never know when it might come in handy."

"That's right," said Mary Margaret. "Bail bondsmen demand cash up front."

It was a Friday night a couple of weeks after the paper drive and the members of Sister Mary Mummy's class were gleefully bouncing off the safety rails, each other, and the cold, lumpy surface of the I Only Have Ice For You Skating Rink. Though less than 20 per cent of us were upright at any given moment, our woeful lack of ice skating skill failed to diminish our enjoyment.

Immediately upon arriving at the dank and dingy establishment on the outskirts of La Bamba we had stormed the counter *en masse* clamoring for skates while entertaining private visions of speeding across the rink on flashing silver blades. We got the skates alright, but with only one or two notable exceptions, our visions went unfulfilled.

Sullivan's experience was fairly typical. After strapping on his skates he had fallen four times *before* reaching the ice. Taking no such chances, "Fat" Chance elected to crawl to the skating surface on his hands and well-padded knees. I was watching his slow but safe journey when Marty Shea poked me in the ribs.

"Look at Dudley," he whispered, gesturing towards

the forlorn figure slumped alone on a bench near the skate rental counter.

"Yeah," I whispered back, "it's sad."

Dudley's loudly stated and oft-repeated reason for remaining benchbound was that he didn't want to take the chance of aggravating an old ankle injury. The *real* reasons behind his reluctance to join us, however, were many and varied.

He was still sulking about the fact that he had lost the $50 paper drive prize to a kid in the sixth grade. Though everyone was shocked by that unexpected turn of events, Dudley was positively devastated. He had arrived at school that miserable Monday morning perched triumphantly upon a gigantic mound of newspapers piled in the back of his father's pickup truck, and had greeted our transparently insincere congratulations for accumulating what appeared to be the winning poundage with totally uncharacteristic humility.

"Looks like you mugged half the newspaper boys in La Bamba," joked Marty Shea as we helped Dudley and his father unload the truck.

"How'd you know that?" hissed Dudley.

We were still unloading the Mack's truck when an even bigger truck pulled up in the front of the school. Its entire bed was crammed with newspapers that rose higher than the roof of the cab. Additionally, several bundles were lashed to the fenders. Not since the Joad family left the dust fields of Oklahoma for the orange groves of California had a vehicle been more heavily, more *precariously* loaded.

Dudley was still reeling from the unexpected loss of the 50 big ones when he suffered a second blow.

"All right, class," Sister Mary Mummy had said that afternoon, shortly after the eighth grade had been declared the winning class, "I am open to suggestions regarding the class outing you have earned."

"I vote for an evening at the ice rink," said Mary Margaret Delicate.

"That sounds like F-U-N," shouted Suzy Fondell, Our Lady of the Gulag's one and only sex symbol. Suzy, who wanted to be a professional cheerleader almost as badly as Mary Margaret Delicate wanted to be a nun, had this maddening penchant for turning everything she said into a victory cheer.

"How about a slumber party?" said Sullivan, leering at Suzy.

"A camping trip!" yelled someone else.

"Skiing!" said another.

"A trip to The Museum of Natural History!"

"A movie!"

"Vegas!"

"*What?*" said Sister Mary Mummy.

"Vegas," repeated Dudley Mack. "You know, Las Vegas. It's a— "

"Yes, I do know what it is, Mr. Mack," said Sister Mary Mummy. "I also know *where* it is. Unfortunately, our meager budget precludes out-of-state travel. Please try to think of something a little more local."

"O.K.," said Dudley. "How about Europe? I ain't never been there."

"I *haven't* ever been there," corrected Sister Mary Mummy.

"Well, if you ain't been there either what'dya say we check it out?"

We eventually narrowed our choices down to two: ice skating and a weekday movie matinee. The final vote was 16 for the former, 13 for the latter, and one abstention. Dudley refused to cast a ballot after Sister Mary Mummy summarily removed Vegas and Europe from contention.

He didn't refuse to accompany us on the outing though. Despite his announced intention of boycotting the trip, no one was especially surprised when he boarded "The Yellow Peril," Our Lady of the Gulag's ancient school bus, for the crosstown run to the rink.

"Good evening, Mr. Mack," said Sister Mary Mummy from behind the wheel of the roughly idling bus. "I certainly hope you aren't planning to hijack us to Europe."

"No, S'ter," mumbled Dudley, settling himself into a nearby seat. He leaned back and closed his eyes, a clear indication that he wasn't going to participate in the festive horseplay that surrounded him.

Dudley's aloofness continued when we reached our destination, although he did break his self-imposed silence long enough to individually inform each member of the class that he was going to remain on the sidelines because of a bum ankle.

Displaying the sensitivity of Martin Bormann, Sullivan responded by saying, "Hey Dud, how can your ankle still be sore? I pulled that thorn out months ago."

The fact that Dudley didn't respond to Sullivan's remark indicated the severity of his sulk. There was nothing wrong with his ankle of course, and his anger at having been upstaged by an upstart sixth-grader, as well as his frustration over the outing election, had only a little to do with his decision to assume the role of spectator. The main reason behind his refusal to don the blades was fear—fear of making a fool of himself in an athletic endeavor. Though a superb athlete, Dudley was astute enough to realize that his chances of gliding gracefully around the rink his first time on skates were roughly equivalent to Sullivan's chances of being unanimously elected "Most Popular" by his classmates.

The fact that Mary Margaret Delicate was now performing Sonja Henie-like maneuvers in the center of the rink while surrounded by an admiring group of fellow students only compounded Dudley's misery and cemented his resolve to stay right where he was. Mary Margaret, who had practically grown up on ice skates, was certain to comment on Dudley's proficiency or, more accurately, his lack of same, should he venture out onto the slick ice. He wasn't about to subject himself to *that* indignity.

Marty Shea and I were mildly surprised to discover that we were unable to truly enjoy ourselves while Dudley was sitting there by himself.

"I can't really put my finger on it," Marty said, "but somehow I feel like a traitor being out here while he's over there."

"Me too," I agreed. "But what can we do about it? There's no way we're gonna talk him into joining us."

"I know. The only thing we can do is join him."

A few minutes later we plopped down on the bench with Dudley.

"What a dumb sport," said Marty with a theatrical sigh.

"Yeah," I said quickly, "and Dudley was the only one who knew that without trying it."

Dudley didn't acknowledge us.

We were desperately trying to think of something else to say when Sister Mary Mummy approached us.

"Hello, boys," she said. "Why aren't you skating?"

"We were," responded Marty, "but we decided to take a little break."

"I see," said Sister Mary Mummy. "And what about you, Mr. Mack? It appears that you are lacking certain essential apparatus."

"Huh?"

"Skates, Mr. Mack," she said, indicating his loafered feet. "You aren't wearing skates."

"Ah, they didn't have my size," lied Dudley.

"Nonsense. What size do you wear?"

"13, I guess."

"Hey, buddy," yelled Sister Mary Mummy to the obviously bored man at the rental counter, "you got any 13's back there?"

"Yes, ma'am. Got two pairs of 13's."

"Perfect," said Sister Mary Mummy. "That's my size, too." She grabbed Dudley by the arm and lifted him off the bench. "Let's grab those blades and show them how it's done," she said.

Ignoring Dudley's hysterical claims of suffering every disease and ailment known to mankind, Sister Mary Mummy quickly got them both into skates. She then began half-dragging, half-carrying the protesting Dudley towards the rink. The wobbly procession of the nun, the reluctant skater, and Marty and me attracted considerable attention, and a crowd gathered near the railing to see what was going on.

"Please, S'ter," Dudley whispered frantically, "don't make me go out there. I ain't never been on skates before."

"Neither have I," she said. "Looks like we're going to learn together."

The crowd at the railing, which included the entire eighth-grade class and most of the rink's Friday night regulars, parted like the Red Sea as Dudley and Sister Mary Mummy stepped onto the ice to begin their first circular journey. Though their progress was extremely slow and shaky, they completed the trip without falling once. A round of applause greeted them as they glided past the gathering at the rail, and Sister Mary Mummy acknowledged same with a wave of her hand and a slight bow. With each successive circumnavigation of the rink they became less shaky and visibly more confident. Gradually the rest of us joined them on the ice, and Dudley and the nun simply became two skaters among many.

After skating side-by-side for several more revolutions, Sister Mary Mummy announced that she was going to sit down and rest for a while.

"Care to join me, Mr. Mack?" she asked.

"No way, S'ter," he said. "I'm havin' too much fun."

"Very well," said Sister Mary Mummy, "but take it easy. You aren't Dick Buttons you know."

"Who?"

"Never mind," said Sister Mary Mummy, exiting the

ice.

Of course Dudley paid absolutely no attention to her advice. Though his skill level was improving steadily, his confidence level was positively skyrocketing. He had become fairly adept at making wide turns, but short, quick turns and stopping were still well beyond his ability. Typically, Dudley wasn't about to let a little thing like that stop him from going full out.

"How about a five-lap race?" he said.

"It's against the rules, Dud," replied Marty Shea.

"I know. That's what gave me the idea."

"Count me out," said Marty.

"Ditto," I said.

"Sissies!" shouted Dudley, sprinting away from us.

He repeated the epithet moments later when he sped past us on the turn. Then, as he entered the straightaway, it happened. While attempting to show off, Sullivan had collided with Mary Margaret Delicate and Suzy Fondell, causing all three of them to fall in a tangled heap... directly in Dudley's path!

I winced in anticipation of the horror that was imminent, and gruesome scenes of severed limbs flashed in front of me. Suddenly, from out of nowhere, I saw a black blur streaking across the ice with skates spitting ice like those of an N.H.L. wing on a breakaway charge. Sister Mary Mummy's mad dash was designed to intercept Dudley before the impact. It didn't appear that she had a chance, but miraculously she got there in time.

Even more miraculously, she swept Dudley off the ice and *lifted him over her head* in one smooth motion. The tips of his blades missed Sullivan's head by a fraction of an inch.

Mary Margaret, Suzy, and Sullivan were saved by the incredible maneuver, but now Sister Mary Mummy and Dudley, not to mention several innocent skaters, were in grave danger.

Still holding Dudley over her head, Sister Mary

Mummy somehow managed to weave in and out of the passing traffic like a Grand Prix driver on a crowded track. After barely missing the final startled skater that stood between her and the safety rail, Sister Mary Mummy applied the brakes ... hard. A rooster tail of shaved ice shot 15 feet into the air as she came to a halt at the edge of the rink.

"Perhaps you would like to sit down for a while after all," she said to Dudley Mack, gently lowering him onto the ice.

Though too shocked to respond verbally, Dudley's eyes answered in the affirmative.

On the ride home we asked Sister Mary Mummy how she was able to perform such an amazing feat.

"Well, the way I figure it," she said softly, "God protects drunks, little children and nuns on ice skates."

"Amen to that," said Dudley Mack.   ❧

V

THE
HALLELUJAH
HOOPSTERS

H, OH," said Marty Shea, "I don't think the coach is gonna like this a bit."

"Not unless he has a crepe paper fetish," murmured Jimmy Sullivan.

Dudley Mack didn't say anything. He just stood there staring in disbelief at the hideously festooned gymnasium.

Meanwhile, the blue-fingered members of the Student Decorating Committee were busily unfurling even more rolls of the crinkly crepe streamers that approximated Our Lady of the Gulag's school color, and taping them to the few places in the tiny, pre-Spanish/American War gym that had thus far escaped decoration. The persistent draft that wafted through the ancient structure caused the miles of streamers already in place to undulate, giving the distinct impression that a gigantic ocean wave had somehow been loosed in the building.

Sullivan, whose stomach was almost as weak as his character, was suddenly overcome with an attack of nau-

41

sea and he left hurriedly.

Mary Margaret Delicate, the chairman of the Decorating Committee and one of the few Our Lady of the Gulag students who could legitimately claim a high degree of literacy, climbed down off the rickety ladder that was being supported by a couple of her flunkies. "There," she announced, "all we have to do is cover those wooden boards and hang a few streamers from those iron rings with the silly nets."

While her crew stood around congratulating themselves on their handiwork, Mary Margaret Delicate approached us.

"How does it look?"

"Like a bunch a crepe," replied Dudley Mack, slamming a basketball against the warped gym floor and glaring at Mary Margaret. Dudley hated her because she always got straight A's and dotted her "i's" with intricately-drawn little butterflies. Mary Margaret hated Dudley because he usually misspelled his name and consistently lowered the class grade curve.

"What's this all about, anyway?" asked Marty Shea, indicating the garishness that was practically engulfing us.

Mary Margaret Delicate was incredulous. "You mean you don't know?"

"If I knew," Marty Shea replied slowly, "chances are I wouldn't have asked you."

"Well," said Mary Margaret haughtily, "we are decorating the gymnasium for the school dance tomorrow night."

"Are you going to be a chaperone again?"

She was on the verge of assaulting Dudley with a heavy, metal tape dispenser when the flimsy doors of the gym burst open and Coach DeWolf entered.

"OK, guys," he bellowed, "quit standing around and get to work. We have a big game coming up and ..."
Coach DeWolf, Our Lady of the Gulag's basketball coach

and the most feared person on the staff next to Sister Mary Mummy herself, suddenly noticed that his precious gymnasium had been slightly modified.

"Who's responsible for this?" he bellowed. "Who TP'd the lousy gym?"

When no one moved or spoke, the livid coach shoved his silver whistle into his mouth and blew a sharp blast.

"Maybe you didn't hear me the first time," he said, "I want to know who's responsible for this... stuff."

"She is," Dudley said, pointing an accusing finger in Mary Margaret Delicate's direction. Tears were beginning to well up in Mary Margaret's eyes and she took two tiny steps backward in a pathetic gesture of self-defense as Coach DeWolf approached her.

"Did you put this junk up in my gym?" he asked.

"Yes. I, uh, I mean, we did. The Student Decorating Committee did."

"Who is in charge of the Student Decorating Committee?" demanded Coach DeWolf.

"I am," Mary Margaret Delicate whispered.

"Great," replied the coach, smiling brightly. "Then you're just the right person to head the committee I'm forming."

"I am?" gushed Mary Margaret. Next to term papers, her favorite thing in the whole world was committees.

"Yeah," continued Coach DeWolf, "I'm forming the Student *Undecorating* Committee. You have exactly two minutes to get rid of this garbage."

Mary Margaret's fright immediately turned into anger and she refused the appointment in no uncertain terms. "We were authorized to put up these decorations for the school dance," she said. "and we're not going to remove them."

"What twisted idiot authorized you to disrupt basketball practice in *my* gym?" thundered Coach DeWolf.

"I guess I'm the idiot you're referring to," said Sister Mary Mummy. Her arrival in the gym had gone totally unnoticed.

"Gee, Sister, I, uh, I..."

"Now what seems to be the problem, Mr. DeWolf?," said Sister Mary Mummy. She addressed the embarrassed coach as "Mister" because he was an ex-student of hers and she always addressed her male students, past and present, as "Mister." She never called him "Coach" because that was his given name; Coach DeWolf was named after Coach Knute Rockne of Notre Dame, a man Coach's father idolized.

"Uh, there's no real big problem here, Sister," mumbled Coach DeWolf. "I have just requested that the young lady and her staff remove the crepe paper so that we may have our regularly scheduled basketball practice."

"I know your team needs all the practice it can get," said Sister Mary Mummy, "but couldn't you just work on dribbling or fouling while the Decorating Committee finishes up?"

"With all due respect, Sister, I don't think so. I was planning an intra-squad scrimmage today and we can't possibly have one if the baskets are crammed with crepe."

"I don't see why not," said Sister Mary Mummy evenly, "I've seen your boys play and they haven't ever come close to putting a shot into the basket."

Coach DeWolf was really getting exasperated now. "C'mon, Sister. Just tell your Committee to back off. I'll even compromise and let the mess that's already up stay there if you'll keep them away from my baskets."

"I realize that the Sistine Chapel's in no danger," replied Sister Mary Mummy, "but to dismiss the fine efforts of the Student Decorating Committee as a "mess" is uncalled for. Personally, I find the decorations to be quite attractive."

"Hey, I thought nuns weren't allowed to lie," whispered Dudley Mack.

Finally, Sister Mary Mummy broke the impasse with a suggestion that was at least as bizarre as the surroundings in which we found ourselves.

"I'll tell you what," she said with a gleam in her eye, "the Student Decorating Committee and I will play you and your team in a 15-minute scrimmage. If we win, the decorations will be removed. If you somehow manage to defeat us, your practice will yield to the decorations. Fair enough?"

"But the Student Decorating Committee is all girls. You wouldn't have a chance."

"We'll worry about that," said Sister Mary Mummy firmly.

"C'mon, Coach," Dudley Mack pleaded. "We'll cream 'em. With you at center, they don't stand a chance."

"OK," said Coach DeWolf finally, "but who'll call the fouls?"

"Our consciences," said Sister Mary Mummy. With that, she led her squad to the far end of the floor for a pep talk. It was only then that we noticed she was wearing a squeaky-new pair of high-topped basketball shoes and a pair of black wristbands.

During our allotted five-minute warmup we shot at about 15% primarily because of Coach DeWolf's amazing consistency. He had been the best player in Our Lady of the Gulag's history and he had even been drafted by the Pistons after college, but his pro career had ended almost before it began because of his tendency to make mental errors. Major ones, and a lot of them. Like showing up at the wrong arena on game days, and blocking free throws—his teammate's free throws.

At the other end of the court, Sister Mary Mummy was hurriedly explaining the game of basketball to her team while attempting to teach them a few rudimentary patterns to run. Naturally we were quite confident that we would win. Our confidence got a tremendous boost when one of Sullivan's spectacularly errant passes ac-

tually dropped through the hoop. It was the first time he had made a basket in his life, and it prompted talk of a possible shutout.

"We're ready," shouted Sister Mary Mummy.

"OK, guys," said the coach," let's go get 'em."

Since we didn't have a referee, we decided to let Sister Mary Mummy's team inbound the ball. Mary Margaret Delicate awkwardly tossed it to Sister Mary Mummy, who began dribbling purposefully towards our defensive alignment. Crossing the center line, she suddenly dipped her left shoulder and drove toward the top of the key. As Coach DeWolf stepped out to meet her she stopped, pump-faked him off his feet, and then leaped straight up. Her unmolested jumper swished into the net, causing the coach to swear under his breath. As Marty and I brought the ball down the court, we noticed that the Sister had deployed her troops into a loose zone defense. Marty pulled up on the left side and rifled the ball to Dudley, who was cutting across the lane. From out of nowhere, Sister Mary Mummy's hand reached out and caught the bullet pass as easily as an All-Star third baseman might gather in a soft line drive. Instantly, she became a black blur racing down the middle of the court. Dudley was angling to cut her off when she took off from just behind the foul line. Holding the ball firmly in her right palm, Sister Mary Mummy executed a perfect slam dunk as Dudley ran completely *under* her. We were down four-zip.

I brought the ball down the right side and lofted a soft, alley-oop pass to Coach DeWolf. Sister Mary Mummy was all over him, so after a few ineffectual attempts at driving the lane, he dribbled toward the outside, head-faked once, and executed a beautiful left-handed hook. Though caught completely off balance, Sister Mary Mummy recovered in time to partially block the shot, tipping the ball toward Mary Margaret Delicate, who was being guarded by Dudley Mack. Mary Margaret grabbed the ball and immediately passed it back to Sister Mary Mummy. Their game plan was now obvious. The nun was going to be their entire offense.

We regrouped under our basket and waited for her. She was bringing the ball up court very slowly while whispering instructions to Mary Margaret. Smiling, Mary Margaret nodded at Sister Mary Mummy and trotted to her position near the left corner. Once again, Sister Mary Mummy drove towards the top of the key, but this time she didn't bother to try to fake the coach. Instead, she went up with the ball and since our entire team went up with her, we didn't see Mary Margaret standing all alone under the basket.

Sister Mary Mummy did though, and she threaded a perfect pass between the leaping Coach DeWolf and a befuddled Dudley Mack. Mary Margaret Delicate made it 6-0.

We couldn't believe it. Sister Mary Mummy was all over the court, blocking shots, stealing passes, and sinking soft jumpers from practically the next block. And somehow her makeshift team was able to dominate the defensive boards by hanging back and letting us bat the ball into their waiting hands. After that it was a simple case of feeding the Sister for two.

With about a minute-and-a-half left in the game, we were down 14-6, but things were finally starting to go our way. We scored six quick points in a row, including two by Dudley Mack who managed to drop in a layup on a brilliant, body-control drive. 14-12.

There was less than half a minute left to play and we had the ball.

"One shot," screamed Coach DeWolf. "Let's go for that one sure shot."

Marty and I went into a stall, playing catch near the center line. Sister Mary Mummy was getting edgy and she kept moving closer to us.

"Now," screamed the coach, breaking towards the

basket. Marty's pass led him perfectly and Sister Mary Mummy was caught out of the play. Tie game, 14 apiece.

"Eight seconds," yelled the student who had been drafted as the official timer.

Mary Margaret Delicate got the ball in to the Sister who was being pressed by Coach DeWolf.

"Three seconds," screamed the timer as Sister Mary Mummy went up for a desperation jumper from just inside the baseline at *our* end of the court. With a flick of her powerful right wrist, she released the ball over the outstretched hand of the coach.

"Time!"

Everyone on the court stood motionless as we watched the ball disappear into the layer of blue crepe paper that hung twenty feet over the court.

"It'll never make it," said Dudley. "Nobody can shoot a full-court jump shot. Nobody."

"Don't be too sure," cautioned Marty Shea. "She's pretty strong."

Dudley was about to say something else when the ball suddenly dropped through the crepe paper ceiling at the far end of the court. We watched in open-mouthed awe as it hit the rim and bounced straight up. Seconds later, it dropped cleanly through the net.

"Will I see you boys at the dance tomorrow night?" said Sister Mary Mummy, grabbing a few rolls of blue crepe streamers with one hand and a ladder with the other.

We were, of course, too stunned to answer.   ❧

VI

FLY NOW, PRAY LATER

HE DECIBEL LEVEL inside the *Yellow Peril*, a rolling detention cell that served as Our Lady of the Gulag's school bus, had long since passed the medically acceptable maximum and it showed little sign of diminishing. Nearly two dozen of us had boarded the decrepit vehicle a few minutes earlier. Since our destination was a ski resort instead of a stuffy classroom, our collective mood was far more buoyant than the one we usually carried on board. Besides the high level of excitement, we had also brought along a supply of ski paraphernalia that ranged from the exotic and the expensive to the makeshift and the, in at least one case, stolen. Late arrivals, faced with the task of negotiating the cluttered aisle of the bus, ran a grave risk of being skewered by a casually discarded ski pole.

The circumstances that led to our presence on the school bus that Saturday morning had begun several weeks earlier.

"Before we make another undoubtedly futile attempt

to gain an understanding of the intricacies of the English language," Sister Mary Mummy had said one cloudy November morning, "I have an important announcement to make."

"They've extended Lent," someone murmured.

"The cafeteria's lima beans finally killed somebody," mumbled another voice.

Sister Mary Mummy, oblivious to the whispered speculation, continued, "As you know, the eighth grade class goes on a winter outing every year..."

"...and the Class of '58 never returned," muttered Marty Shea.

"...and this year is no exception. In fact, we have arranged a special trip for this class."

She paused and I noticed that even Dudley Mack, Our Lady of Gulag's token incorrigible, was paying attention, a rare occurence indeed.

"You," said Sister Mary Mummy dramatically, "are going to Purgatory!"

Instantly, Dudley Mack was on his knees.

"Please, Sister," he wailed, "not the big P. I promise I'll never carve my initials in another church pew. Just give me one more chance. Please."

Confused by Dudley's desperate plea for mercy, Sister Mary Mummy reacted as any eighth-grade teacher might: she began to call the roll. By the time she reached the *F*'s, her composure had returned.

"What's this all about, Mr. Mack?" she demanded.

"I'm not ready for Purgatory," he moaned.

"Well, I'm sure they have some beginner's slopes."

"Beginner's slopes?"

"Certainly. Most ski resorts do, you know."

"Dudley," said Marty Shea quietly, "I think Purgatory is a ski resort, not a..."

"I knew that all along," interrupted Dudley with a nervous laugh.

Now, from our encampment on the rear seat of the

Yellow Peril, Marty Shea and I exchanged surprised looks as the hulking figure of Dudley Mack approached. We were surprised because he was only a few minutes late despite the fact that he had developed tardiness to a high art, the result, he claimed, of being the product of an induced birth. Dudley was wearing a blindingly bright green parka and matching stretch pants.

"What an ungodly hour," he said.

"You're almost on time, Dud," said Marty Shea. "What happened?"

"I underslept," Dudley said. "But I did forge my permission slip," he added proudly.

"Hey Dudley," called the unmistakable voice of Jimmy Sullivan from somewhere near the back of the bus, "that's a cute outfit. Does the Jolly Green Giant know it's missing?"

Dudley, who was large enough to have masqueraded as a three-story building the previous Halloween, lunged toward Sullivan. Since it was obvious that he wasn't planning to congratulate him on the cleverness of his remark, Marty Shea and I tried to restrain him. Sullivan, suddenly aware that his life was in danger of premature termination, began screaming in terror. Our fellow passengers began scrambling over skis, seats and each other, hoping to catch a glimpse of the action.

Sister Mary Mummy chose that exact moment to board the bus. She quickly surveyed the chaotic scene and then brought her open hands sharply together. The resulting thunderclap froze the action and cut Sullivan off in mid-scream. Later, we discovered that it had registered a 4.5 on the Richter Scale.

"He was trying to hit my fist with his mouth," said Dudley in an attempt to establish his innocence. Sister Mary Mummy didn't buy it for a minute.

"Mr. Sullivan, I want you to sit up here near me. Mr. Mack, you sit in the back. The rest of you may sit anywhere, ... *after* the skis and poles are placed safely under

the seats."

Her instructions were carried out efficiently and with all due haste.

"Fine,"said Sister Mary Mummy, easing herself into the driver's seat. "We're on our way. Enjoy yourselves."

Only the fun-loving, irrepressible and thoroughly dislikeable Sullivan responded to her invitation. He began singing the traditional, going-skiing-by-bus-traveling-anthem, "A Hundred Bottles of Beer on The Wall." Fortunately, Sister Mary Mummy's patience was less well-rounded than her rumored 360-degree peripheral vision.

"Knock it off, Sullivan," she ordered, before he was midway through the first verse. We applauded her decision lustily and Sullivan promptly commenced a deep sulk.

A few hours later, the majestic Mount of The Holy Cross came into view. The 14,000-foot peak's rock and snow formations form a natural cross that is said to deepen the religious fervor of many who view it.

"That's my favorite mountain," said Sister Mary Mummy.

"How come?" asked Sullivan.

Not surprisingly—some would even say, fittingly—Sullivan was destined to become the outing's first and only casualty. Shortly after Sister Mary Mummy guided the *Yellow Peril* into the parking lot at Purgatory, Sullivan, with all the coordination of a newborn flamingo, entangled his legs in his skis as he was leaving the bus, and fell off the bottom step. He broke his right ski in three places and his left leg in four.

While Sister Mary Mummy accompanied our fallen comrade to the local emergency hospital, the rest of us went off to challenge Purgatory's slopes.

Though I had never been on skis before, I managed to put on my rented boots without seriously injuring myself, and only a brief struggle was required to get the boots locked into the bindings. Dudley and Marty, both

of whom shared my lack of experience, also fared well,
and we shuffled off to the beginner's slope.

My visions of flashing down a steep, mogul-infested
run, trailing a gigantic rooster tail of powder promptly
evaporated when I saw the beginner's hill, a treacherous
expanse of snow that had been christened *Demon*.

"I have seen hell and it is in Purgatory," muttered
Marty Shea.

"Let's rent a toboggan," Dudley suggested as a five-
year-old sailed off a small mogul nearby and expertly sla-
lomed between us.

"Good idea."

We were nearing the bus when we ran into Sister Mary
Mummy. She was carrying Sullivan's four skis and his
boots.

"How's ol' Jimmy?," we asked, hoping our lack of con-
cern was not apparent.

"He's fine," she answered. "His parents are on their
way to pick him up. Are you boys through skiing already?"

"Yes, Sister. Skiing doesn't seem to be our sport."

"That's too bad," she said. "It certainly looks like fun."

"Say there, S'ter," said Marty, "why don't you try it?
You can use Dudley's skis."

"Yeah," said Dudley, glancing at her sturdy shoes.
"you don't even need boots."

"I don't know..."

"C'mon, Sister."

She eventually gave in, agreeing to try a short run, and
she soon had her shoes firmly locked into the bindings
on Dudley's skis. "I'll need some gloves," she said. Dudley produced a pair of gaudy mittens emblazoned with
the Coors beer logo. She pulled them on without comment.

When we returned to *Demon*, Sister Mary Mummy began to sidestep up a gentle part of the slope. Thirty yards
up the hill she stopped, adjusted her grip on the ski

poles, and glided back to where we stood.

"That was fun," she announced. "I think I'll try it again."

This time she *walked* to a point 75 yards up the slope and added a slight flourish to her stop when she returned. Her excitement was obvious and she spent the next hour experimenting with slow turns and the hill's mild moguls. By mid-afternoon, she decided she had outgrown *Demon* and was ready for a bigger challenge.

The grizzled, old chair lift operator was incredulous.

"I ain't never seen a nun ski before," he said.

"You have now," replied Sister Mary Mummy, settling into a chair.

Despite the large number of skiers populating *Lower Hades,* the slope's official designation, Sister Mary Mummy stood out easily. None of the other skiers were wearing habits. We anxiously followed her progress as she gracefully crisscrossed the trail on the way down. Showering us with a spray of snow, she spun to a stop five feet away. "Once more," she said. "with a little *style* this time."

Moments later, she was again rocketing down *Lower Hades* when she suddenly changed course and disappeared into a cluster of trees.

"She's heading for *Mogul Alley,*" someone gasped.

Sure enough, Sister Mary Mummy was airborne when she emerged from the trees. After touching down, she made an immediate turn and lifted off a mogul of imposing size and sheerness.

"Look at that!" screamed Dudley Mack.

Sister Mary Mummy had drawn her skis close to her body and was beginning to roll forward. She was in the tuck position 15 feet above the sloping surface.

Miraculously, she completed the forward flip and landed upright. Instantly, she went into a low crouch and sprung off a small jump. At the peak of her ascent, she performed a beautiful front flip in the layout position and then, almost as an afterthought, added a perfectly executed full twist.

No one spoke as she skidded to a stop in front of us.

"Is there a big jump around here?" she asked. "I've gotta catch more air."

The seldom-used 90-meter ski jump provided all the air she needed. She began her flight with a halftwisting, full gainer. The brisk wind seemed to catch the folds of her habit and hold her up as she flew through the air *backwards*. Suddenly, she formed a cross with her skis, held it momentarily, and then managed a full layout back flip with a half twist at the top. The successful completion of that maneuver coincided with her gentle landing on the hard-packed snow.

Obviously heavily influenced by the movie *Ben-Hur*, Sister Mary Mummy ended her one-woman winter carnival performance by commandeering two toboggans and riding them Roman-chariot style through the intricate giant slalom course.

During the long ride home I couldn't shake the notion that I had heard the good Sister humming "Nearer My God To Thee" while she was sailing through the air after taking off from the ski jump, but I finally decided the wind had been playing tricks with my imagination.   ∾

VII

THE HOLY ROLLERS

MARTY SHEA, Our Lady of the Gulag's primo nun-spotter, saw her first.

"Over there," he said. "Lane 24."

Dudley Mack and I peered through the gloom of Coogan's Bowl in the direction indicated by Marty's pointing forefinger. Sure enough, Sister Mary Mummy was ambling toward the scoring table on Lane 24. A pair of bowling shoes whose dimensions were exceeded only by their gaudiness were slung over her left shoulder.

"Good work, Marty," I said.

"Thanks," he mumbled. He was justifiably proud of his ability to sense the presence of any nun within a hundred yards. It was a unique and valuable skill that had saved us on more than one occasion.

"Check out those shoes," whispered Dudley Mack. "If Liberace was a cowboy, those would be his saddlebags."

"Yeah," said Marty Shea, "but at least they don't clash with basic black."

"I didn't think nuns were allowed to go bowling," said Jimmy Sullivan.

"Sure they are," I said. "They're always looking for an excuse to get out of the convent and into the alleys."

We had ended up hanging out at Coogan's Bowl that Saturday afternoon more by accident than design. Originally, we had planned to spend the day at the movie theater next door shooting paper clips at Elvis Presley and dripping hot butter onto the heads of those patrons who had chosen not to sit in the balcony. Unfortunately, the manager of the theater *had* elected to sit in the balcony and we were apprehended before the first paper clip was even halfway to the screen. Marty Shea's powers did not extend to detecting the presence of theater managers.

After spotting Sister Mary Mummy we realized it just wasn't our day. Our adolescent sensibilities told us it would be wise to leave immediately, but the prospect of watching a nun bowl was too good to pass up. The fact that Sister Mary Mummy was accompanied by Sister Superior, her boss at Our Lady of the Gulag, and Monsignor Munchkin, cemented our decision. We decided to stay.

Dudley Mack sauntered over to the soft drink machine while Marty and I unobtrusively slid into a booth a few lanes from where Sister Mary Mummy was changing into her bowling shoes. We tried not to stare at her for fear that a direct glance would alert her to our presence, but after a few minutes it was apparent that we were being overly cautious. Both nuns were focusing their full attention on Monsignor Munchkin, who was conducting an impromptu bowling clinic. He was explaining the function of the bowling ball when Dudley joined us.

"This is the ball," Monsignor Munchkin was saying, "and those are the pins."

"OK," said Sister Mary Mummy and Sister Superior.

"The object of the game is to knock down as many pins as you can with the ball," continued Monsignor Munchkin.

"That sounds easy enough," said Sister Superior brightly.

"It's harder than it sounds, Sister."

"I'm sure it is," giggled Sister Superior.

"Now," continued the Monsignor, "you get two tries at the ten pins. If you knock them all down with the first ball, that's a strike."

"Strike," repeated the nuns reverently.

"If some pins are left standing after the first ball and you get them with the second ball, that's a spare."

"Spare," repeated the nuns.

"OK," said the Monsignor, "grab your balls and let's go."

Sister Mary Mummy and Sister Superior, guided by the nervous little priest, approached the ball rack. Although both nuns were wearing their dress uniforms, the Monsignor was attired in a pair of baggy green slacks and an orange and blue bowling shirt that had the words "Pin Buster" stitched across the back. He was also wearing his familiar Bing Crosby-style porkpie hat and he had an unlit pipe in his mouth. Monsignor Munchkin's admiration of Bing was well-known, as was his love of the movie "Going My Way."

In fact, a few weeks before, while conducting our annual sex education class, he had ended his lecture with a passionate plea against "going my way." After our initial confusion, we realized that he meant "going *all* the way," a euphemism for what we assumed was something that fell into the category of major heaviness.

When Monsignor Munchkin returned to the scorer's table and began penciling in the names of the competitors, Marty Shea grabbed my arm.

"Look," he said. "Do you see what I see?"

"I think so," I stammered. Dudley Mack indicated that he, too, saw what was happening by choking on his root beer.

Sister Mary Mummy had just wrapped her hand around a

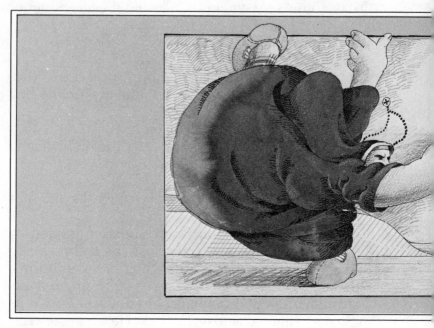

16-pound bowling ball and was carrying it toward the ball re-
turn like it was a softball!

"This ball is damaged," she said loudly. "It has three
holes in it." She returned it to the ball rack.

"They're *all* damaged," she said.

"No, they're supposed to have three holes, Sister,"
said Monsignor Munchkin. "The holes are for your
thumb and fingers. Like this," he said, demonstrating
the proper grip.

"Oh," mumbled Sister Mary Mummy. "Of course."

Meanwhile, Sister Superior, a tiny woman who was to
Sister Mary Mummy what a seedling is to a giant red-
wood, was struggling with a ten-pounder. She had already dropped it several times and was now fighting to
place it on the ball-return carousel. She almost made it,
when the ball slipped off and landed on her right foot.
She closed her eyes and glanced heavenward.

"Father?" she said softly.

"Yes, Sister?" answered Monsignor Munchkin, who was unaware of her misfortune.

"This game sucks," said Sister Superior.

"What's wrong, Boss?" asked Sister Mary Mummy.

"The damn ball fell on my foot. I'm afraid I'll have to sit this one out."

"Are you all right?"

"I'm fine," said Sister Superior as Sister Mary Mummy carried her to the bench with one hand.

Sister Mary Mummy experimented with her grip while Monsignor Munchkin rolled first. He threw a slow-rolling hook that got a lot of action but left a defiant ten-pin. He failed to pick up the spare.

"I always start slowly," he said apologetically. "Your turn, Sister."

Sister Mary Mummy stepped up to the line and eyed the fresh array of shiny pins 60 feet away. After a brief hesitation, she began an awkward stutter-step toward the foul line. When she was about three feet away, she swung her right arm in a complete arc and released the ball, which sailed toward the pins at a tremendous velocity. It was about six inches off the ground the whole way, and when it crashed into the head pin it sounded like a thunderclap. All ten pins vanished immediately.

"A strike my first time," said Sister Mary Mummy happily. Monsignor Munchkin sat motionless at the scorer's table.

"That ball never even touched the alley," whispered Dudley Mack. *"It was a line drive!"*

The Monsignor was so shaken that he buried his next two balls in the gutter.

"How unfortunate," said Sister Mary Mummy. "Two sewer balls."

"Gutter balls," corrected the Monsignor.

"Whatever," said Sister Mary Mummy.

She plucked her ball from the carousel and took her position at the top of the lane. Again, she approached the foul line with all the grace of a right tackle dancing "Swan Lake," and again she released the ball at the tail end of a windmill delivery. Seconds later, all ten victims of her felonious assault were cartwheeling from sight.

"Beginner's luck," mumbled Sister Mary Mummy, who had removed from bowling the need to read surfaces.

A crowd began to gather around Lane 24, and we left the booth to join them.

Monsignor Munchkin shuffled up to the line and half-heartedly rolled his ball. The Brooklyn hit resulted in an agonizingly slow pin dance that eventually turned into a strike. He appeared not to notice.

"C'mon, Sister," screamed Sister Superior from the bench. "Put 'em away."

Sister Mary Mummy responded with her third strike in a row.

"Congratulations, Sister," said Monsignor Munchkin.

"A turkey."

"I beg your pardon, Father."

"A turkey, Sister. Three strikes in a row is called a turkey."

"Quaint," said Sister Mary Mummy.

By her next time up, she was playing to the rapidly growing gallery.

"I've already got a turkey," she said loudly. "Here comes the stuffing."

Enthusiastic applause greeted her fourth strike, and Sister Mary Mummy responded with a theatrical bow from the waist.

She continued to throw a strike every time she laid her hands on the ball, but Monsignor Munchkin's game was becoming increasingly erratic. He was bowling like an out-of-control marionette, and the little feather in his hat had begun to droop.

Nearly a hundred people had congregated at Lane 24 by the time Sister Mary Mummy was preparing to bowl in the tenth. She had tallied nine straight strikes; three more would give her a perfect game.

"Pop them pins," screamed Sister Superior.

Sister Mary Mummy gave her the thumb's up sign and got number ten. She nonchalantly dried her hand over the blower as she waited for her ball to return. When it arrived, she plucked it from the carousel and walked to the head of the lane *tossing* the 16-pound weapon lightly from hand to hand. The crowd gasped and seconds later strike number 11 was history.

Sister Mary Mummy was but a single strike away from a perfect game her first time out!

The crowd became silent as she addressed the pins for the final time. Sister Superior was fingering her rosary, and the beaten Monsignor had removed his Bing Crosby hat and was holding a lit match over the end of his pipe, which had somehow become inverted.

Sister Mary Mummy stood at the top of the lane for a

long time before commencing her final approach.

"Too early," breathed Dudley Mack as she started her arc. "She's too early."

Sister Mary Mummy suddenly realized that she had indeed begun her arc too soon, so she quickly inserted two more steps into her approach and completed the windmill motion without releasing the ball. Her momentum was carrying her closer to the foul line and it seemed certain she would foul.

At the last moment, she swung her arm in a *second* arc and released the ball perfectly. It sailed towards the pins on its silent, clothesline trajectory and exploded into the head pin. A mad scramble took place at the far end of the lane and all the pins disappeared from sight.

Except one!

The eight-pin was fighting to remain on the surface of the lane. It was spinning crazily and an eternity passed before the recalcitrant pin began to slow down. Finally, it stopped spinning completely and a collective groan issued from the crowd.

Then suddenly and without warning, the pin *split in half*. After the briefest pause, the left half of the bisected pin toppled over, but the right half remained rooted in its upright position.

Sister Mary Mummy had bowled a 299½ game!

It was the last time she ever bowled, and, as far as I know, she is the only person in the long and glorious history of the sport to have felled nine-and-a-half pins with a "double arc" delivery.

Of course, the crowd was understandably disappointed that she failed to get her perfect game, but Sister Mary Mummy was philosophical about it.

"The Lord giveth," she said, "and the Lord taketh away. It's just that occasionally He forgetteth to taketh it *all* away."

VIII

AMAZIN' GRACE

HANKS LARGELY to Mary Margaret Delicate's natural gift for verbally dispensing information of little or no consequence to vast numbers of people in practically no time at all, word of Sister Mary Mummy's bingo victory spread faster than a brush fire in a gale. Less than 12 hours after Monsignor Munchkin called out the final number at the parish's weekly Tuesday night game, the entire Our Lady of the Gulag student body knew that B-13 had given Sister Mary Mummy a blacked-out card—bingo's version of the grand slam—in the evening's cover-all finale.

Most of us greeted this news with an equanimity that was based on either a profound lack of understanding of achievement or an equally profound lack of interest in it. Dudley Mack's reaction was, of course, attributable to the former.

"So she blacked out, huh?" he said, interrupting Mary Margaret's breathless monologue. "I didn't even know she drank."

"Actually, Dud," said Marty Shea, "I don't think she does. When Mary Margaret mentioned a blackout she was referring to Sister Mary Mummy's bingo card, not her physical condition."

"Oh."

Though Mary Margaret was obviously horrified that anyone, even the cretinous Dudley Mack, could be so blatantly sacrilegious as to mention a nun and demon alcohol in the same breath, she pulled herself together and resumed her narration. "Anyway," she said, "not only did she—"

"Wait a minute," blurted Dudley. "I ain't never heard of no St. Bingo."

Tears of rage and frustration instantly filled Mary Margaret's blue eyes at this second interruption of her oral report in less than a minute.

"That's because there is no St. Bingo," said Marty. "We aren't talking about holy cards, Dud."

"We aren't?"

"Nope."

"Are we talkin' about baseball cards?"

"Afraid not."

"Playin' cards?"

"No."

"Well if we ain't talkin' about holy cards, baseball cards, or playin' cards, what the hell kinda cards *are* we talkin' about?"

"*Bingo cards*, you dumb moron," shrieked Mary Margaret, momentarily forgetting her vow never to speak to Dudley. "We're talking about *bingo cards*."

"Well, why didn't you just say so in the first place?" asked Dudley innocently.

Fury contorted Mary Margaret's semi-placid features into an ugly mask and she lunged at Dudley's throat. Jimmy Sullivan and I were somehow able to grab her before she reached her intended target, and we began to drag her south. Marty quickly took Dudley's arm and gently guided him northward. By the time the avowed enemies were safely separated, Mary Margaret realized she had grossly violated her rigid code of personal behavior and she struggled to regain control of her emotions. She hadn't been this upset since the time Sister Mary Mummy publicly ridiculed her for dotting her i's with intricately-drawn butterflies, calling them a pathetic affectation.

While Mary Margaret tried to get a grip on herself, Marty carefully explained the nuances of bingo to a thoroughly bewildered Dudley. He also made Dudley promise not to disrupt the bingo tale if and when it should continue.

Several minutes later, a cool, calm, collected Mary Margaret was babbling away as if nothing had happened, and Dudley was miraculously honoring his promise to keep his trap shut. He remained mute while Mary Margaret rehashed the part about how her father, "the top aluminum siding salesman in the world," had insisted that Sister Mary Mummy allow him to buy her a four-bit bingo card, and he didn't say a word when she theatrically approximated the nun's supposed reaction at the moment of victory. But Dudley broke both his silence and his promise when Mary Margaret casually mentioned the $250.

"$250?" he roared. "What $250?"

"Tell him," Mary Margaret instructed Marty.

"Uh, that's how much she won, Dud."

"Won? You mean they weren't playin' for fun?"

"Are you kidding?" asked Sullivan. "Fun is for amateurs. When it comes to bingo, Catholics are pros all the way."

"But that's gamblin'."

"Technically you may be right," said Marty, "but—"

"—but nothin'," thundered Dudley. "I know what is gamblin', an' I know what ain't gamblin'. I also know that in this state gamblin' happens to be illegal." He paused and looked directly at Mary Margaret. "That means," he said slowly, "that our beloved teacher is, at this very moment, an unindicted felon, a fugitive from justice. One little phone call to the D.A.'s office and they'll lock her up for —"

"She isn't a criminal," screamed Mary Margaret.

"No one is," said Dudley evenly, "until they're caught."

At that moment the bell calling us to class rang, but Dudley's prosecution and Mary Margaret's spirited defense of Sister Mary Mummy continued until we were within a few feet of the defendant's classroom.

As usual, Sister Mary Mummy had stationed herself outside the classroom door to greet each of her students individually.

"Good morning, Mr. Sullivan."

"G'mornin', S'ter."

"Good morning, Mr. Shea."

"Morning, S'ter."

"Good morning, Miss Delicate."

"Good morning, Sister, and how are you this fine day? Did you notice that the birds seem to be chirping especially brightly and that —"

"Good morning, Mr. Mack."

"Howdy. What are you gonna do with the money you won?" Dudley was nothing if not direct.

"So you've heard about my recent good fortune?" said Sister Mary Mummy.

"Nope. But I did hear about how you won 250 bucks playin' bingo last night."

"I see."

"So what are you gonna do with it, send it to the Pope or somethin'?"

"Why in the world would I send it to the Pope?"

"So you won't mess up your vow of puberty."

"Vow of poverty, Mr. Mack."

"Whatever."

"All right," said Sister Mary Mummy, "since the subject has been raised with such subtlety and tact, I will tell all of you this much: I have made what I consider to be a very fine investment with my winnings."

"Good Lord," whispered Marty, "she's already spent it. Talk about money burning a hole in the ol' habit pocket."

"Did you buy municipal bonds?" asked Mary Margaret. "They're tax-free, you know."

"Yes, I do know, Miss Delicate," replied Sister Mary Mummy, "and no, I didn't buy muni bonds."

"Debentures?"

"With a capital investment of $250, less commission? Be serious."

"I know," squealed Suzy Fondell. "You bought the cheerleader squad new uniforms and pom-pons."

"Fat chance of that," said Sister Mary Mummy.

"C'mon, S'ter," the class whined, "tell us. Please."

"You'll find out soon enough," said Sister Mary Mummy with a mysterious grin. "Just be patient."

∿

Bright and early one Saturday morning a few weeks later Dudley, Marty, Sullivan and I were shooting baskets in Marty's driveway when Mary Margaret and Suzy rode up on their bikes.

"You'll never guess what just happened," shouted Mary Margaret, executing a graceful dismount from her shiny, red Schwinn.

"They just discovered that excessive neatness kills?"

"No," said Mary Margaret, ignoring Marty's sarcasm. "Sister just called me on the phone. At home."

"Huh?"

"Sister just called her on the phone," repeated Suzy in the peculiar cadence generally associated with cheerleaders everywhere. "You know, give me an F, give me an O, give me an N, give me..."

"We *know* what a phone is," said Marty. "Why did she

call is the question."

"I-Don't-Knowwwww," cheered Suzy. "Why did she call, Mary Margaret? C'mon now, don't be shy, stand up and tell us why."

"Suzy, if you don't knock off that insipid cheerleader crap," said Mary Margaret, "I'm personally going to rip your stupid pom-pons apart, pom by silly pon."

"I can't help it," replied Suzy defensively. "It's in my blood. Every time I see a football I just have to cheer."

"But this is a basketball," said Sullivan.

"Oops. I wondered why you guys weren't wearing helmets."

"Anyway," said Mary Margaret, returning to the business at hand, "Sister told me she could use your help for an hour or so this afternoon at one o'clock."

"Help to do what?"

"I'm not sure. She didn't say. I would go myself, but I have to iron my shoelaces."

"Well, you can count me in," said Sullivan.

"Yeah, I guess I can spare an hour," said Marty. I indicated that I would be there as well.

"Fine," said Mary Margaret. "But what about him?" She pointed at Dudley.

"It ain't exactly polite to point at folks, M.M.,"Dudley said, "but I'll let it go this time."

"How about it, Dud? You with us?" asked Marty.

"Yeah, I'll be there. I already ironed *my* shoelaces."

"Good," said Sullivan, "it'll be a lot of fun."

"I'll be the judge of that," said Dudley Mack.

At precisely one o'clock we rolled into Our Lady of the Gulag's sorry excuse for a playground.

"Where is she?" muttered Dudley as we secured our wheels to the bike rack next to the ancient drinking fountain that dispensed a lukewarm substance that resembled nothing so much as liquid rust.

"Over here, gentlemen," shouted Sister Mary Mummy. She was casually leaning against a half-dozen enormous cardboard cartons that had been deposited near the entrance of the dilapidated gymnasium, a facility that made the Black Hole of Calcutta look like a garden spot by comparison. We approached her slowly and carefully.

"Thanks for coming on such short notice," she said. "I was expecting this to arrive on Monday, but they crossed me up and delivered it two days early."

"What is it?" asked Dudley as he strolled around the pile of boxes. "Or them?"

"It's the little investment I told you about a while back," replied Sister Mary Mummy. "As you boys know only too well, our gymnasium equipment is neither plentiful nor is it in especially good repair."

"Gee," said Marty, "I was always under the impression that if a gym had the tattered remnants of a volleyball net and two peach baskets nailed to warped plywood backboards, it had just about everything."

"Your sarcasm is appreciated," said Sister Mary Mummy, "because it happens to be quite justified. Or perhaps I should say, 'it *was* justified.' But as of this moment, the gymnasium facilities at Our Lady of the Gulag have taken a giant step into the 20th century." She slapped her palm against the side of the box nearest her. "And for that we may thank the contents of these cartons."

"Terrific," shouted Sullivan. "You bought us a new volleyball net, and some real backboards with real metal hoops and cord nets, and a basketball that doesn't have to be inflated between dribbles, and —"

"Hold on there, Mr. Sullivan. I'm afraid I've bought none of those things."

"As in not a single one?"

"That's correct. However, I did buy something much, much better. Something that every single student at this school will be able to enjoy for years to come.

"So this is what 250 bucks worth of comic books looks like," muttered Dudley incredulously.

"Sorry to disappoint you, Mr. Mack," said Sister Mary Mummy, "but it isn't comic books. It is ... gymnastics equipment."

"*Gymnastics equipment?*"

"Right. Of course it's used, but I got an incredible deal on it. We now have a balance beam, a sidehorse, a high bar, a dozen mats, and not one, but two sets of parallel bars—even and asymmetrical. They even offered to throw in a trampoline, but I decided it wouldn't be very practical in a gym with a 15-foot ceiling."

"*Gymnastics equipment?*"

"I knew you'd be as thrilled as I am. Come on, let's get this stuff set up so we can try it out."

❧

Three hours and much under-the-breath grumbling later, we had everything in place.

"You boys did a magnificent job," said Sister Mary Mummy as we stood in the middle of the sagging gym floor and surveyed the exotic apparatus that surrounded us. She was being overly-generous with her praise since she performed approximately 100 percent of the actual labor.

"Thanks, S'ter," mumbled Marty, Sullivan and I nonetheless.

Apparently Dudley wasn't interested in accepting the unearned compliment. "It looks like a jungle gym blew up in here," was all he said.

"To the untrained eye perhaps," said Sister Mary Mummy, "but put a skilled gymnast on any piece of apparatus in this room and you'll soon see feats of artistry and sheer beauty unsurpassed by any sport I'm aware of."

Dudley walked over to the side horse. "You mean to tell us that crawlin' around on this horizontal tacklin' dummy with handles is a *sport*?"

"Those are called 'pommels', Mr. Mack, not handles, and yes, it is indeed a sport."

And with that, Sister Mary Mummy reached into the folds of her habit and pulled out a wrinkled paper bag. She dipped her right hand into the bag and withdrew what appeared to be a handful of powdered chalk. Vigorously rubbing the stuff into her palms, she said, "I'm extremely rusty, but I'll try to show you what I mean."

When she was sufficiently chalked, Sister Mary Mummy approached the side horse and wrapped her massive hands around the pommels. Drawing a deep breath she then executed a flawless front scissors mount and commenced a series of full leg circles. Her brief side horse routine ended with a feint to a three-quarter double leg circle and a triple rear dismount. At least that's what she said she'd done and we were certainly in no position to dispute her.

"How'd you learn all that junk, S'ter?" asked Dudley with undisguised admiration.

"Mostly from books," replied Sister Mary Mummy, reaching down to adjust the soft gymnastics slippers she was wearing. "I also had a chance to watch Shakhlin, the superb Russian gymnast, demonstrate his impressive side-horse skills a few years ago and I learned a lot from him. Of course my little performance was but a pale imitation of his, an exceedingly pale one."

We tried to believe her of course, but we couldn't. Because we had absolutely no basis for comparison, we were convinced that Sister Mary Mummy was the best gymnast in the history of the civilized world. Our conviction grew even stronger during the next hour or so as we watched her bound from one piece of equipment to another demonstrating her remarkable prowess on each.

She did a number of picturesque giant swings on the high bar, scraping plaster from the ceiling with her feet on each revolution; she did back flips on the even parallel bars; she did front flips on the balance beam; and she did aerials, handsprings, and back walkovers on the tumbling mats. But the most incredible exercise she performed before her appreciative, properly-awed audience of three that afternoon took place on the uneven parallel bars. After running through a brief, fast-paced routine, she somehow ended up standing on the upper bar with her back to the lower bar. Hesitating for a brief moment, she then leaped straight up. It appeared that her head was going to collide with the ceiling, but she went into a tight tuck immediately after leaving the bar and began revolving like a 4th of July pinwheel.

Her triple front somersault was over in the wink of an eye. It was a truly spectacular maneuver, but she made it infinitely more spectacular by adding two-and-a-half twists before catching the upper bar and swinging her body into the lower bar to finish with what we later discovered was a cast-wrap Hecht dismount.

"I guess that's enough for one day," she said when we finished applauding.

"Couldn't you just show us a few simple moves before we go?" asked Marty.

"Yeah, Sister," whined Sullivan. "Please."

Even Dudley asked for some rudimentary instruction, which indicated that Sister Mary Mummy's enthusiasm for gymnastics was indeed infectious.

Unfortunately, our first group lesson ended almost before it began when Sullivan badly sprained his wrist trying to do a simple forward somersault on the mats, and for some reason we never quite got around to a second lesson. In fact, we never again had anything to do with the gymnastics equipment, unless you want to count the night Dudley broke into the gym and did 25 chin-ups on the high bar to win a bet.

Sister Mary Mummy continued to work out regularly, however. She must have, because although there was a serious, unexplained chalk shortage at Our Lady of the Gulag the rest of that year, the front of her habit always showed traces of the stuff.   ᷜ

IX

THE STINGING NUN

HAD'YA THINK she's gonna do?" Jimmy Sullivan's lips were quivering like a bowl of Jello on a fault line and his eyes advertised sheer terror.

"Oh, not much," replied Marty Shea offhandedly. "I'm sure she'll merely thank the officer for escorting us back to school and then give us all A's for destroying public property."

Sullivan, his senses almost totally dulled by the imminent prospect of facing Sister Mary Mummy's towering wrath, responded to Marty's sarcasm by uncharacteristically lapsing into silence.

"Can you believe that jerk?" Marty whispered.

"No," I replied, "but then I can't believe we've been arrested either."

"Well, we have," chimed in Dudley Mack, a veteran of more than a few such inconveniences.

It was true. We had been nabbed by the long arm of the law a few minutes earlier, shortly after a firmly packed,

grapefruit-sized snowball propelled by the strong arm of
Dudley Mack had connected with a car windshield, shat-
tering same.

That the vehicle happened to be a police cruiser dramatically worsened our predicament, as did the fact that
we were on traffic-patrol duty at the time of the soon-to-
be-infamous Snowball Sniping Incident.

Not surprisingly, our feeble protestations of innocence
failed to impress the irate officer who had taken us into
custody.

"We was buildin' us a midget snowman," said Dudley,
unlimbering his unique flair for fiction, "an' I was about
to put a tiny head on its little body when I dropped it."

"Let me get this straight," said the incredulous cop.
"You accidentally dropped a midget snowman's head in
such a way that it traveled horizontally some 40 feet with
sufficient force to shatter my windshield?"

"Right," Dudley beamed, obviously pleased with the
originality of his lie.

"Wrong," shouted the cop, herding us toward the
damaged cruiser. Along the way, he casually mentioned
that a number of motorists had called the precinct that
morning to report they had been bombarded by snowballs in the vicinity of Our Lady of the Gulag. "Fact is,"
he continued, "I was on my way to investigate the alleged
allegations which are, of course, no longer mere allege-
ments."

Though we were only a few blocks from school, the
journey to the imposing brick fortress took nearly 15 minutes because while it's not particularly easy to navigate a
vehicle through a blinding snowstorm under normal circumstances, it is doubly difficult when the windshield
has more cracks in it than a dry river bed.

Immediately upon arriving at our destination Sullivan
went completely around the bend and assumed the fetal
position in the back seat of the cruiser. Only the threat of
an additional charge of resisting arrest got him uncurled

and on his feet.

That accomplished, we commenced our reluctant procession toward Sister Mary Mummy's temporary headquarters. Sister Superior, the regular principal, was out of town at a teachers' conference, and Sister Mary Mummy was Acting Principal. She was also the commandant of Our Lady of the Gulag's crack crossing-guard corps, an organization whose carefully nurtured image we had just destroyed.

"Good morning, Officer," said Sister Mary Mummy as we paraded into Sister Superior's closet-like office. "What seems to be the probl—"

"I didn't do it," Sullivan screamed. "They made me do it. I didn't mean to do it. I'll never do it again, I promise."

Obviously confused by Sullivan's hysterical outburst, Sister Mary Mummy just stared at him. Finally, she found her voice. "Please let the officer explain why he brought you here, Mr. Sullivan. We'll have plenty of time for your denials or confessions later on."

"Well, Sister," said the policeman, "these four Caucasian males are the suspected perpetrators of a series of 312's—unprovoked assaults on vehicular traffic with elements of nature."

"Could you kindly put that into plain English?" requested Sister Mary Mummy.

"Sure. These punks broke my windshield with a snowball."

"I see," said Sister Mary Mummy evenly. "Are you absolutely positive there's been no mistake? I mean, I can't believe that anyone, even these gentlemen, would be stupid enough to throw snowballs at a police car."

"There's no mistake, Sister. They did it."

"We didn't know it was a cop car," blurted Dudley. "It was snowin' so hard we couldn't see nothin'."

After collecting the names and phone numbers of our parents, the officer gave us the old "I-won't-take-you-in-this-time-but-don't-let-it-happen-again" lecture. Sister

Mary Mummy then thanked him for escorting us back to school.

"Well, I was half right," mumbled Marty Shea. "She did thank him."

"I don't want to hear any lame excuses or silly fabrications," Sister Mary Mummy said when we were finally alone. "The broken windshield on that squad car adequately states the case against you."

Sullivan started to say something, but Sister Mary Mummy quickly cut him off.

"Put a lid on it, Mr. Sullivan."

"I just wanted to—"

"I said, 'Put a lid on it!'"

"Yes, S'ter."

"And keep it there."

"Yes, S'ter."

"Now, as I was saying, your actions of this morning seem to demand some sort of disciplinary action, don't

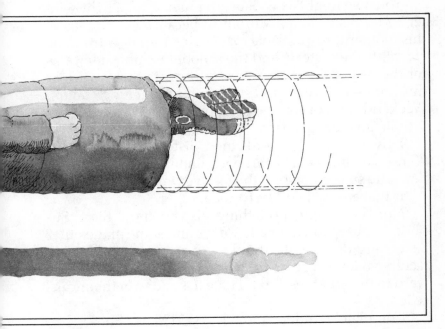

they?"

"Depends," said Dudley, failing to grasp the fact that if there ever was a rhetorical question, Sister Mary Mummy had just asked it.

"And since your parents will undoubtedly have to bear the financial responsibility for your little escapade," she continued, ignoring Dudley's overt foolishness, "that punishment should be quite severe, shouldn't it?"

By now, Dudley had come to the realization that Sister Mary Mummy wasn't interested in establishing a dialogue on the matter and he joined the rest of us in nodding assent.

"Fine," said Sister Mary Mummy. "We'll begin by having each of you turn in your crossing guard badges, which I see are tarnished literally as well as figuratively."

After a bit of nervous fumbling, we managed to remove the tin shields from our heavy coats and handed them over.

"You also might as well begin praying for a light winter," said Sister Mary Mummy, "because you are, as of this moment, responsible for clearing the snow from the convent, the rectory, and the school-building sidewalks for the rest of the year. You may perform that particular duty either before or after school or on your lunch hours. Weekends are, of course, excepted."

Sullivan meekly raised his hand. "Driveways, too?"

"Driveways, too," confirmed Sister Mary Mummy. "Since you boys enjoy throwing snow around so much, I'm quite sure you'll find the task very rewarding."

"Is that all?" asked Marty Shea.

"No. There's one more thing. As you know, Sister Superior is out of town for a few days and some of the other Sisters are down with the flu. As a result, our weekly faculty volleyball game is short a few players. I look forward to those games and I'd hate to see one of them cancelled."

"Completely understandable," said Marty Shea.

"Good," said Sister Mary Mummy. "I'll see you in the gymnasium after school this afternoon."

We turned to leave, but she had one final comment. "It's stopped snowing so I'm sure you'll put the noon hour to good use. The shovels are in the custodian's closet."

Dudley was the first to speak once we were out of Sister Mary Mummy's earshot. "I ain't playin' no volleyball with no nuns," he said. "No way."

"I don't like it either," said Marty, "but there's no telling what she'll do if we don't show up."

"He's right," ventured Sullivan. "We got off pretty easy so far. Let's not mess it up."

Later that afternoon we entered the dark and drafty Our Lady of the Gulag gymnasium. A half-dozen nuns, each clad in a pair of well-worn sneakers, were gently hitting a volleyball back and forth across the holey remnants of a volleyball net that had obviously seen better days. We felt as out of place as a flame paint job on a Rolls Royce.

"Thank you for clearing the snow from our sidewalk, boys," called Sister Mary Bigfoot, the genial sixth-grade teacher.

"Our pleasure, S'ter," replied the perpetually diplomatic Marty Shea.

A few moments later, Sister Mary Mummy strode into the gym. She was followed by a sweat-suited Monsignor Munchkin, the kind-hearted, incredibly clumsy parish priest.

"I wonder whose windshield *he* broke," Dudley Mack whispered as the Monsignor self-consciously waved at us.

"O.K., gang," shouted Sister Mary Mummy, "let me have your attention. With the kind assistance of Monsignor Munchkin and some of my students we have our usual dozen."

The Sisters applauded politely and Monsignor Munchkin blushed deeply.

"And," continued Sister Mary Mummy, "Sister Mary Bigfoot has graciously consented to join forces with the men for tonight's game, so let's get this show on the road."

Within minutes we were involved in a warmup rally that lasted until Dudley made contact with the ball for the first time. If we had been playing in Yankee Stadium, Dudley's drive would have easily reached the centerfield monuments.

"Dudley, old boy," said Monsignor Munchkin, "save your power until you're in the front line. I have a feeling we're going to need it."

The game commenced with Sister Mary Mummy delivering six straight service winners. At least two of them were long, but Dudley ignored our shouts to let them go and punched them into the ceiling ... hard. Finally, on the seventh serve, she faulted.

Monsignor Munchkin quickly got us back into the game with his tricky serves and an assist from Dudley, who contributed two perfect sets that Marty Shea managed to dump over Sister Mary Primo's attempted blocks. A nice firm spike by Sister Mary Primo, however, ended our comeback attempt at five points.

With the serve out of Sister Mary Mummy's hands for awhile, we played the nuns evenly. Though our lack of teamwork and skill was hurting us, we compensated with a lot of hustle. At 10-11 theirs, Sister Mary Mummy and Dudley found themselves at the front line center for their respective teams. Marty served a moon ball to Sister Mary Cantakerous in the right corner and she bumped it cross court to Sister Mary Martin, who executed a beautiful set to Sister Mary Mummy. Uncoiling her large frame, Sister Mary Mummy leaped straight up, and swung her right arm in a vicious downward trajectory. The resulting spike sped past Dudley's ineffectual block, but it was out by three feet. Our point, 11-11.

A combination of luck and more luck gave us the next three points before Sister Mary Mummy gave the ball another ride. This time it caught the corner. 11-14.

We got the serve back without allowing a point, but gave it up when Sullivan served into the bottom of the net. Sister Mary Mummy then stepped to the service line and unleashed a twisting line drive that went untouched for an ace. Sullivan bumped her next two offerings into the bleachers and we were tied at 14-apiece.

Unaccountably, Sister Mary Mummy's serve suddenly deserted her, a fate that next visited Monsignor Munchkin. Neither team was able to produce any points and we found ourselves rotating like two rotary engines.

The score was still tied when Sister Mary Mummy got the serve back once again. She responded with another clean ace. The only contact on the play occurred when Monsignor Munchkin and Dudley Mack collided in their scramble to reach the ball.

"Game point," called Sister Mary Mummy, preparing to serve another one.

A long and spectacular rally, easily the best of the afternoon, ensued. The ball crossed the net at least a dozen times as members of both teams contributed a dazzling array of miraculous shots and impossible retrievements. Unfortunately, Sullivan somehow got himself entangled in the rickety bleachers during the heat of the battle, which left us one player short.

"Medic!" he shrieked, holding his right knee. Dudley finally noticed Sullivan's predicament, but instead of rushing to his aid, he rushed forward to take Sullivan's place at the net.

Upon seeing this maneuver, Monsignor Munchkin set the ball to Dudley, who authored a truly prodigious spike that rocketed toward an open area on the other side of the net. It looked like a sure winner, but out of the corner of my eye I saw Sister Mary Mummy fling herself at the ball. She looked like an oversized torpedo as she left her feet and flattened herself out over the warped hardwood floor. Reaching the ball just before it touched down, she sent it straight up into the air. Then, in one smooth motion, she rolled over her right shoulder and leaped to her feet.

Sister Mary Primo, normally a precision setter, positioned herself under the rapidly descending sphere and prepared to set it to Sister Mary Mummy, who was now at the net. It was a piece-of-cake play at this point, but for some reason Sister Mary Primo's set angled *away* from the net, toward her own team's baseline. Sister Mary Mummy took off after the ball, running a little loop to the left before converting her substantial horizontal motion into a vertical one. A sound not unlike a small explosion resounded throughout the gym as her massive right hand made contact with the ball. She was spiking from *behind* her own baseline.

Too stupified to react, we stood motionless as the long-distance spike sailed across the net into fair territory and ricocheted into the wall at the far end of the gym.

Sister Mary Mummy's amazing feat on the volleyball court that day was overshadowed only by the the fact that for the rest of the winter it only snowed on Saturdays and melted by Monday morning.   ～

X

SWING LOW, SWEET FASTBALL

LTHOUGH IT WAS still very early in the morning, we were already sweltering in the hermetically sealed classroom located in the maximum security wing of the fortress known as Our Lady of the Gulag. Even Mary Margaret Delicate, who prided herself on the fact that she didn't know how to sweat, was feeling the effects. The stiffly starched collar of her uniform was beginning to curl, and her meticulously combed and sprayed flip was starting to droop. Of all those present in the stifling room, only Sister Mary Mummy showed absolutely no signs of discomfort, despite the fact that she was wearing enough black, heat-absorbing fabric to outfit a dozen undertakers and still have enough left over to retain if not clerical, at least secular modesty. Her apparent obliviousness to the heat only confirmed the widely-held suspicion that her cold heart pumped ice water rather than blood through her veins.

Sister Mary Mummy was simultaneously looking for

signs of subversive activity among her 30 prisoners and
delivering a lecture on the relative merits of the various
coordinating conjunctions.

I, meanwhile, was mentally calculating the odds of our
rapidly diminishing oxygen supply holding out until the
noon recess. Upon concluding that they were something
less than favorable, a parade of banner headlines swam
before my eyes.

"30 Students Found Asphyxiated In Classroom; Nun
Accused Of Gross Negligence" seemed most appropriate for the home edition, so I wrote it on a piece of paper
and passed it across the aisle to Marty Shea when Sister
Mary Mummy turned to assault the blackboard with a
handful of chalk. Marty quickly scribbled something on
my note and passed it back to me.

"Better make that 29 students," he had written.

He was right of course. It had been more than an hour
since we had marched, alphabetically and in single file,
into the classroom, and Dudley Mack was still missing.
Dudley was always late, but seldom more than five or ten
minutes, and he rarely missed an entire day. That this
was the day on which he normally collected his weekly
protection money from the entire seventh-grade class
only made his absence all the more alarming.

Suddenly the vault-like classroom door flew open and
Dudley Mack himself burst into the room.

"Uh, oh," muttered Marty Shea, "he doesn't look very
happy."

Indeed he didn't. Though Dudley's normal disposition alternated between sullen and angry, he appeared
to be in a rage of monumental dimensions. Without so
much as a glance towards Sister Mary Mummy, whose
dust-spewing labors at the blackboard had been infer-
rupted by his entrance, Dudley stomped down the aisle
and quite literally threw himself into his desk. A deathly
silence enveloped the room as we held our collective
breath in anticipation of the confrontation that was

imminent.

A long moment passed before Sister Mary Mummy spoke. "Well," she finally said, "what was it this time, Mr. Mack? Did you find it necessary to stop on the way to school to rescue some helpless orphans from a blazing inferno? No, of course not. How silly of me. That was yesterday's excuse. Perhaps you had to escort your poor mother to the hospital on the bus for another in a long series of major operations? Or maybe you got up early this morning to study and became so enthralled by the finer points of English grammar that you completely forgot about the time? On second thought, the burning orphan story is more plausible. So tell us, Mr. Mack, what unique disaster did you meet with today? Please don't keep us in suspense."

Dudley didn't answer. He just sat there glaring at the nun in the chalk-streaked habit.

"We're waiting, Mr. Mack," cooed Sister Mary Mummy. "Aren't we class?"

"Yes, S'ter," we chorused obligatorily.

"Let's just say I was, uh, derailed," said Dudley wearily.

"Derailed? How utterly inventive. There's not a locomotive within 20 miles of here and yet you managed to get yourself derailed on the way to school."

"You know what I mean," sputtered Dudley, his face reddening even further. "I was de, uh, de..."

"De*tained*," whispered Marty Shea.

"...de*tained*," said Dudley Mack.

"Thank you, Mr. Mack," said Sister Mary Mummy, "and you too, Mr. Shea. Now I would appreciate it if one of you gentlemen—preferably you, Mr. Mack—would kindly tell me exactly why you were detained."

"Somebody stole my bike," mumbled Dudley.

"We can't hear you, Mr. Mack. Can we, class?"

"No, S'ter."

"I said, '*Somebody stole my damn bike!*'"

Instantly a wave of horror swept over the class and Mary Margaret Delicate began screaming. That anyone would be stupid enough to steal anything from Dudley was shocking enough, but for him to yell at Sister Mary Mummy, and to use a swear word besides, was almost too much for us to comprehend. That had to be a capital offense at the very least. Dudley Mack was surely going to be executed right before our eyes!

To our surprise, however, Sister Mary Mummy merely smiled at Dudley's outburst.

"Mr. Mack, I do believe that you're actually telling the truth for a change," she said. "In view of that singularly remarkable event, and because it is quite obvious that you are emotionally distraught, I have decided to over-look the fact that you raised your voice to me. However, I have no choice but to punish you for your consistent tardiness. You will remain after school for an hour every day this week."

"But I'll be late for baseball practice," said a subdued Dudley, "and Coach Inconsulata said if I was late one more time he'd kick me off the team."

"Yeah, Sister," piped up Jimmy Sullivan, "you can't get Dud kicked off the 'ol Crimson Tide nine. Our open-ing game against St. John the Other Baptist is tomorrow afternoon and he's our only hope of victory on the dia-mond."

"Sit on it, Mr. Sullivan," said Sister Mary Mummy icily. Then, turning to Dudley, she said, "You mean to tell me that you're habitually late for baseball practice too? I can't justify your classroom tardiness, though I can at least understand it on a philosophical level. But being late for *baseball practice*? That is the most disgraceful thing I ever heard of."

"It runs in my family," said Dudley Mack, lamely. "I can't help it."

"We'll see about that," said Sister Mary Mummy.

With Dudley Mack in the custody of Sister Mary

Mummy, it was a morose group of baseball players who gathered at Our Lady of the Gulag's baseball field later that afternoon. We all knew that Coach Inconsulata had absolutely no intention of kicking Dudley off the team for showing up late at practice. Actually the only thing that might conceivably make him give Dudley the boot would be if the pitcher asked his daughter, Monica Inconsulata, to go steady. Fortunately, that hadn't happened yet, but it was certainly a possibility. Dudley had often threatened to pop the question to Monica and only the fact that he hadn't gotten around to stealing a ring was holding him back. Or so he claimed.

In any event, no one, with the possible exception of Dudley himself, knew better than Coach Inconsulata just how valuable Dudley was to the Crimson Tide. Without him, we were a miserable excuse for a baseball team; with him on the mound, we were a miserable excuse for a baseball team with a tremendous pitcher.

We were discussing Dudley's incarceration among ourselves when Coach Inconsulata finally arrived at the field. Upon spotting the coach's car, Jimmy Sullivan began sprinting towards the parking lot.

"She's got Dudley locked up!" Sullivan screamed at the startled coach. "She's got him locked up! You gotta spring him, Coach. You gotta get him outa there or we're doomed. *Doomed.*"

With the hysterical shortstop on his heels, Coach Inconsulata trotted towards the impromptu team meeting on the pitcher's mound.

"Would somebody please tell me what the hell this jerk is babbling about?" he panted.

"Sure," said Marty Shea. "He's babbling about the fact that Sister Mary Mummy has sentenced Dudley Mack to a week's detention."

"On what charge?"

"Being late to class."

"That's *all*? How many times has he been late?"

"Every single day for approximately seven-and-a-half years."

"So she waits until today to punish him?" moaned Coach Inconsulata. "Boy, that's just great. That's really great. I work my tail off to come up with a decent ball team, and some overzealous nun comes along and blows the whole thing."

"Uh, Coach," said Marty Shea, "with all due respect, I don't think there's any way we could be considered a decent ball team."

"I know that," replied Coach Inconsulata, "but it don't matter. Dudley can beat any team in the league with one hand tied behind his back and a bunch of girls playing behind him."

"That's really a low blow, sir," said Marty Shea. "It may be true, but you have just deeply wounded every single man on this team except Sullivan, who's not bright enough to recognize an insult when he hears one."

"Who cares?" thundered Coach Inconsulata. "I can't worry about you guys now, not with Dudley in the clutches of that pious team-wrecker. She's not going to get away with this!"

"She's not going to get away with *what*?" asked Sister Mary Mummy. She was standing near the backstop while Dudley, the object of the controversy, loitered nearby.

"Oh, hello there, Sister," said Coach Inconsulata. "How nice to see you."

"I'm sure you're thrilled," replied Sister Mary Mummy, approaching the nervous group on the mound.

"Of course I am," said Coach Inconsulata, his voice betraying his sudden nervousness by entering a particularly high register. "It's not often that we welcome visitors to our field."

"No wonder," said Sister Mary Mummy. "Not that many people are anxious to see the National Pastime desecrated."

"You're joking, aren't you, Sister?"

"Mr. Inconsulata," replied Sister Mary Mummy sternly, "there are two things I never, ever joke about and one of them is baseball."

"Of course."

"Now that the formalities are out of the way," she continued, "I would like to discuss Mr. Mack for a moment."

"Terrific," said Coach Inconsulata, relaxing slightly.

"As I understand it, Mr. Mack is a valuable asset to the uh, uh..."

"Crimson Tide," interjected Coach Inconsulata.

"Ah, yes, the Crimson Tide. Tell me, why is a team that wears blue and white uniforms called the Crimson Tide?"

"Coach idolizes Bear Bryant," chirped Sullivan.

"*That* certainly clears it up," said Sister Mary Mummy sarcastically. "Anyway, as I understand it, Mr. Mack is a valuable member of the team."

"The *most* valuable," said Coach Inconsulata enthusiastically. "He has more pitches than a shady used-car salesman. His curve is absolutely, excuse the expression, wicked, and his fastball is really something. Even I can't hit it."

"What do you mean you can't hit his fastball?"

"Just that," said Coach Inconsulata. "Can't touch his curve either."

"But you used to play in the bigs, didn't you?"

"Yeah, Sister, I did. But only for a few weeks. I spent most of my baseball career in the Yankees' farm system. But that was a long, long time ago."

"Still," said Sister Mary Mummy, "I would think that an ex-major leaguer, regardless of how long ago he played or how little, would be able to put some wood to an eighth-grader's tosses."

"I can see where you're coming from," replied Coach Inconsulata," but this kid's hummer is not to be believed."

Sister Mary Mummy mulled this over for a few moments.

"I've got a little proposition for you, Mr. Inconsulata," she finally said. There was a truly malicious gleam in her eyes, a gleam that prompted Marty Shea to nudge me with his elbow and whisper, "I think she's possessed."

"Sure, Sister," said the coach, somewhat uncertainly. "What is it?"

"Well, I'm fully aware of the fact that your opening game is tomorrow afternoon against St. John the Other Baptist and, believe it or not, I don't wish to be the person responsible for causing the Crimson Tide to suffer what will surely rank as one of the most lopsided, humiliating defeats in the annals of the game, a defeat that you have convinced me Mr. Mack here might possibly prevent."

"So you're going to release him from detention?" said Coach Inconsulata. "Thank you, Sister. I really appre..."

"But on the other hand," continued Sister Mary Mummy, ignoring the coach, "I really am in no position to voluntarily commute Mr. Mack's well-deserved sentence."

"So you *aren't* going to release him from detention?" said Coach Inconsulata.

"Not *voluntarily*," replied Sister Mary Mummy. "However, if you and I were to enter into a, shall we say, sporting wager, and if the sole stake happened to be Mr. Mack's freedom, and if I should happen to lose the wager, then I'd be *forced* to release him from detention wouldn't I?"

"I guess so," mumbled the confused coach.

"No you wouldn't, S'ter," said Sullivan. "You could always welsh on the bet."

"Shut up, Sullivan," yelled Sister Mary Mummy and Coach Inconsulata in unison. Sullivan, though quite used to enduring prodigious amounts of verbal abuse, was crushed by the stereo reprimand. He wandered out to center field where he commenced a truly spectacular sulk.

"What kind of 'sporting wager' did you have in mind, Sister?"

"This ought to be good," whispered Marty Shea.

Sister Mary Mummy didn't answer right away. She merely stood at the foot of the pitcher's mound with her arms folded and waited for the rumbling undercurrent of excitement to fade. When it finally became so quiet that all we could hear were Sullivan's plaintive sighs from deep center, she slowly unfolded her arms and pointed dramatically towards the distant center field fence.

"I wager that I, a middle-aged nun—a *girl* if you will, Mr. Inconsulata—who hasn't had a baseball bat in her hands for several decades, can knock one of Mr. Mack's fabled fastballs over the fence right there."

Her pronouncement was greeted by a stunned silence. We were absolutely speechless. Finally, Coach Inconsulata found his voice.

"That's crazy," he said. "It just can't be done."

"Try me," said Sister Mary Mummy. "Just give me three strikes. If I fail, Mr. Mack will become a free man."

"But, Sister..."

"I insist."

"OK," said Coach Inconsulata. "If you insist. Dudley, go get yourself warmed up."

"Right, Coach," said Dudley.

"Oh, and Dudley?"

"Yeah, Coach?"

"Welcome back," said Coach Inconsulata smugly.

"Don't be too sure," cautioned Sister Mary Mummy, striding towards the jumbled pile of bats lying in the dirt next to the third-base dugout.

Several minutes later Dudley finished warming up and Coach Inconsulata called, "Batter up!" He was grinning like a kid in a candy store. Sister Mary Mummy slowly walked towards the batter's box, weapon in hand. Before stepping in, however, she paused to knock the dirt from her shoes.

"Look," someone cried, "she's wearing cleats. Real metal cleats."

"May I take a look at your footwear, Sister?" asked Coach Inconsulata.

"Sure," she replied, "why not?"

Coach Inconsulata bent down to examine her shoes. "These are kind of old, aren't they? Where in the world did you find them?"

"I didn't find them," replied Sister Mary Mummy. "Tyrus gave them to me when he retired."

"Tyrus?"

"Tyrus R. Cobb. Surely you've heard of him?"

"Yes, of course. But how ... *why* did Ty Cobb give you his cleats?"

"He said it was to thank me for helping him with his hitting when he was a kid. We used to play a lot of ball together when we were growing up."

Coach Inconsulata was practically beside himself.

"You actually helped 'The Georgia Peach' with his hitting?" he shrieked.

"A little," replied Sister Mary Mummy. "Mostly I helped him with his base stealing."

"Tell me," Coach Inconsulata whispered conspiratorially, "did he really sharpen his spikes?"

Sister Mary Mummy lifted her right foot. "Feel for yourself," she said.

Coach Inconsulata ran his finger across the spikes, drawing blood immediately. "He did!" he shouted. "He really and truly did!"

"I often told him I thought it was wrong," said Sister Mary Mummy. "I just don't believe violence has a place in sports. He wouldn't listen to me though. He just said, 'There's a big difference between violence and intimidation. Slidin' into second with my spikes up is just my way of intimidatin'. If the jerk don't get himself outa the way, the resultin' violence is his fault 'cause it ain't mine'."

Coach Inconsulata probably would have knelt at Sister Mary Mummy's feet for all eternity if she hadn't said, "Come on, let's get this show on the road."

She stepped up to the plate and motioned for Dudley to take the mound. He was over at first base asking "Fat" Chance who the hell Ty Cobb was anyway.

Sister Mary Mummy was already dug into the batter's box when Dudley toed the rubber and went into his compact windup. Seconds later the ball was blurring towards the plate. From my position at second base I could see that it was low and away, but Sister Mary Mummy lashed out anyway. Though she was a little late, she managed to get a small piece of it. Foul ball. Strike one!

Dudley's second pitch was a blazing fastball into the heart of the stike zone. This time Sister Mary Mummy's prodigious swing missed it entirely. Strike two!

When Dudley again got the ball, he stepped off the mound and turned his back on the batter. He was vigorously rubbing the scuffed horsehide and grinning quite maniacally. After a brief moment he returned to the task at hand, namely getting the ball past the nun just one more time. As he went into his windup a third time, everything seemed to slow down dramatically. Though that pitch was easily among the hardest Dudley Mack had ever thrown, it seemed to float towards the plate. Sister Mary Mummy's swing also looked too slow, too *deliberate*, to have a chance. But there it was, the unmistakable sound of wood making solid contact with a baseball, Ruthian contact. Everyone followed the flight of the ball as it gracefully arched directly over second base and reached its apex somewhere far above Sullivan's open-mouthed stare.

It was easily a full minute after the called shot disappeared over the fence before anyone moved.

"Thank you, Mr. Inconsulata," said Sister Mary Mummy, casually tossing her bat aside. "And thank you, Mister Mack. You have the makings of a fine pitcher."

Sister Mary Mummy then left the field with Dudley Mack in tow.

&

The next afternoon Dudley pitched six perfect innings against a strong St. John the Other Baptist squad. Unfortunately, he was sitting in a classroom with Sister Mary Mummy during the first three innings when Sullivan allowed 18 earned runs to cross the plate, and the Crimson Tide went down to defeat, 18-4.

Oh yeah, and for some reason known only to herself, Sister Mary Mummy became a dedicated follower of our fortunes for the rest of the season.   &

XI

CADDYCHISM

T WAS THE SECOND DAY of spring vacation and we were hanging around the caddie
shack entertaining vague hopes of picking up
a few bucks by lugging someone's golf bag
over Calvary Country Club's semi-lush terrain.

Since it was a slow day, adolescent boredom struck
quickly and Dudley Mack reacted by chasing Jimmy Sullivan across the practice green aiming a well-shaken bot-
tle of lukewarm orange soda. Marty Shea and I passed
the time by reviewing the round of golf we had just completed, an exercise otherwise known as "improving your
lie." Or in our case, lies.

As duly registered caddies at Calvary C.C., we were
permitted to play the course on weekdays provided we
were on by 6:00 a.m. and off by 10:00 a.m. Dudley Mack,
a prodigious but highly erratic hitter, had, as usual,
posted the lowest score. Of course, his practice of declar-
ing a "gimme" and picking up his ball whenever it
landed on the green helped. Though not totally consis-

tent with the objectives of the ancient and honorable sport of golf, his technique effectively eliminated the chances of three-putting. That the rest of us were denied the same privilege was evident in our scores.

"What didja' shoot on the front nine?," Sullivan had asked Dudley Mack as we approached the 10th tee earlier that morning.

Dudley, his brow more deeply furrowed than a freshly-plowed Iowa cornfield, consulted his scorecard. "Let's see," he drawled, "I shot a...28."

"Not bad, Dudley," said Marty Shea in a voice fairly dripping with sarcasm.

"Well," said Dudley Mack modestly, "the hole-in-one helped a lot."

The "hole-in-one" came on the 154-yard fifth hole, a straight ahead par-three. Dudley's towering tee shot had landed some 40 feet from the hole, but rather than trying for a legitimate birdie, he had opted for a self-proclaimed ace.

"Close enough," Dudley had shouted, marking a bold "1" on his card.

"Congratulations," we had mumbled with frighteningly obvious insincerity.

Dudley finished his puttless round with a 55, a mere 19 under par. I shot exactly twice that and Marty Shea came in with a 95. Sullivan's 134 was misleading because he had lost his last ball on 15 and played the final three holes with a water-logged tennis ball he had found in a clump of weeds.

"With a few breaks I could've broken 90," Marty Shea was saying as Dudley Mack closed in on the fleeing Sullivan.

"Yeah," I replied, wincing as at least six ounces of the sticky orange soda caught Sullivan in the back, "and it would have helped if Dudley hadn't screamed 'Look out' every time you swung."

"He said he couldn't help it if he was good at games-

manship," said Marty. "All the same, I was tempted to
..." Suddenly, Marty lowered his voice. "Clergy at three
o'clock," he hissed. "Don't look up."

Out of the corner of my eye I saw the unmistakable
figure of Sister Mary Mummy approaching. She was accompanied by Monsignor Munchkin, Our Lady of the
Gulag's pastor, and two civilians. All were carrying fully-
loaded golf bags, and I could see that Sister Mary
Mummy's feet were ensconced in a pair of brown and
white golf shoes complete with the obligatory tassels.
She bore the heavy golf bag as easily as one might carry
a quiver of aluminum arrows.

"Hello, boys," said Sister Mary Mummy brightly.
"This is a surprise."

"Hello, S'ter," we said to her feet. "Yeah, isn't it?"

"How would you boys like to caddie for us?," asked
one of the civilians.

We almost sprained our tongues in the mad scramble
to fabricate excuses, and all four of us were babbling in-
coherently when the civilian interrupted.

"Five bucks apiece," he said quietly.

"First tee's this way," shouted Dudley Mack, diving
for the man's bag.

I ended up with Sister Mary Mummy's clubs by design—my colleagues' design. They didn't want them and
I happened to possess the slowest reflexes.

"I'm going to require some assistance and guidance,"
Sister Mary Mummy confided as I struggled to shoulder
the bag. "I've never played before."

"I'll do what I can, S'ter," I mumbled. At the first tee I
demonstrated the overlapping grip and briefly explained
some of the nuances of the game to Sister Mary Mummy,
who declined the honor of teeing off first, preferring instead to watch the others.

Each of the three men teed up, performed elaborate
pre-swing rituals, and then sprayed their balls in the gen-
eral direction of the first green.

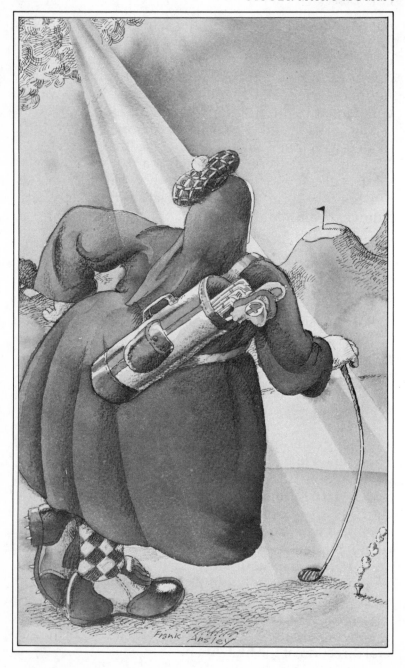

When Sister Mary Mummy bent down to place her ball on the tee, Monsignor Munchkin said, "The women's tee is up there by the red markers, Sister."

"I like this spot just fine," she said, without looking up. Monsignor Munchkin merely shrugged and tossed his driver to Sullivan, who demonstrated the sure-handedness that had made him Our Lady of the Gulag's most inept altar boy.

"Sorry, Father," Sullivan muttered as he retrieved the dropped club.

"Counting you," said the Monsignor, "my handicap is up to 15."

Sister Mary Mummy squinted at the distant flag and stepped up to address the ball. After a lengthy pause she brought the clubface back slowly and chopped at the ball, missing it entirely.

"That's alright, Sister," I said. "Try it again. Just concentrate."

She addressed the ball a second time, paused, and awkwardly slashed at the ball. Again she missed it!

"I'm not doing very well, am I?" she said apologetically.

"You're doing fine, Sister," said one of the civilians. "Just take your time and keep your eye on the ball."

Sister Mary Mummy attacked the ball a third time and again it emerged unscathed. She handed me her driver.

"I've barely begun and I've already struck out," she said.

"No, no, Sister. You get to keep swinging until you hit it," I assured her.

Her fourth effort resulted in a beautiful 325-yard drive down the middle. After a faltering start Sister Mary Mummy had re-established her position as the Babe Didrikson of Catholicism.

Monsignor Munchkin and the two civilians, apparently awed by the Sister's drive, butchered their second shots badly, while Sister Mary Mummy's beautiful approach shot landed 35 feet past the pin. She had to get down in two for a par, but her first putt stopped about six feet short, a difficult distance for even the best players. She marked her ball and stood quietly off to the side as her companions scrambled for triple bogeys and worse.

After they putted out, she replaced her ball on the green and lined up her shot. She stroked it toward the middle of the hole and it looked like it was going to drop, but the ball hit the lip of the cup, spun around the edge and rolled halfway back to where she stood. She stared at the dimpled sphere in disgust and then expertly struck the classic golfer's pose, which consists of a pained expression and eyes cast heavenward. Finally, she put the three-footer away for a bogey and we trudged toward the second tee.

Sister Mary Mummy hit first. Her ball exploded off the tee but hooked dramatically, leaving her with a difficult second shot out of the rough. The other three drives ranged from poor to mediocre and it was obvious that Arnold Palmer and Sammy Snead were in no danger. Nor, it seemed, was Patty Berg.

Though Calvary's front nine was mostly uphill, it was downhill for the Sister all the way. She was making solid contact with the ball, but she had less control than a deposed South American dictator. After one of her high velocity drives tore through a group of trees and landed in an adjacent fairway, Monsignor Munchkin jokingly mentioned something about seeing a squirrel wearing a crash helmet and flak jacket. Sister Mary Mummy replied that one of his "puff shots" wouldn't puncture a spider web.

On the fairways she was carving divots deeper than the kitchen sink and had easily dug up enough turf to re-sod the Los Angeles Coliseum.

I half-expected the waters of the murky pond near the eighth tee to part majestically for Sister Mary Mummy, but her ball disappeared into the murky depths just like the thousands of others that had preceded it. Even the sand traps showed her no mercy.

"I can't believe I actually hit something this small," she said as her drive burrowed into the damp sand of a tiny fairway bunker. She hit out of the bunker and her ball rolled onto and across the green and disappeared over the back edge.

"Uh, oh," I muttered.

"What's wrong?" demanded Sister Mary Mummy.

"Well, Sister," I replied," you're in the biggest, meanest bunker this course has to offer."

As we approached the gigantic sand trap Sister Mary Mummy emitted a long, low whistle.

"There's enough sand here to freak out Lawrence of Arabia," she moaned.

"With all due respect," I said, "it's called *Hell's Half Acre.*"

"Appropriate," she said. "Is there a camel in my bag?"

And, like most novice golfers, Sister Mary Mummy experienced her share of problems on the greens. More precisely, she putted with all the accuracy of exploding shrapnel. After four-putting for about the dozenth time, Dudley Mack quietly suggested that she adopt his "pick-em-up" technique.

"That sounds suspiciously like cheating, Mr. Mack," she said sternly.

"It ain't cheatin', Sister," replied a wounded Dudley Mack.

"It *isn't* cheating," corrected Sister Mary Mummy.

"I know," said Dudley triumphantly, "and it works real good."

By the end of the round, Sister Mary Mummy's entire game, putting included, had improved appreciably. She hadn't exactly mastered golf—no one ever has—but she hadn't succumbed to it either. As I pocketed a fresh $5 bill and watched the intrepid foursome clatter across the asphalt parking lot I couldn't help but notice that Monsignor Munchkin's shoulders were sagging despite the fact that Sister Mary Mummy was carrying his golf bag as well as her borrowed one.

It was understandable though. Monsignor Munchkin had shot a miserable 110. Sister Mary Mummy, meanwhile, had carded a 108.

XII

LET THE
GOOD TIMES ROLL

ISTER MARY MUMMY had a habit of stationing herself just outside her classroom door every morning and greeting her arriving students with an enthusiasm shared only by Marine drill instructors reviewing a busload of new recruits.

We would march past her ramrod stiff figure in alphabetical order, mumbling the obligatory, "G'morning, S'ter," and receiving in return a perfunctory, barely perceptible nod of her head. Once inside the classroom, we would stand at attention beside our assigned desks and await the order to be seated. Like most of my fellow students, I usually spent the first few minutes every morning contending with a slight case of nerve-induced nausea, especially on those all-too-numerous occasions when I had neglected to complete a homework assignment.

If, as many of the students were fond of saying, Our Lady of the Gulag was a prison, Sister Mary Mummy's eighth-grade classroom was surely the maximum security wing. Dudley Mack, in a burst of amazingly uncharacteristic accuracy, had christened it "The Hole" and the appropriateness of that prison analogy would go unchallenged by anyone who had ever heard the magnified echo of finality that sounded when Sister Mary Mummy closed the classroom door. Similarly, the gleam in her eye as she faced her captive charges inevitably brought to mind the self-satisfied expression of a B-movie warden locking the bars on Public Enemy #1.

To describe Sister Mary Mummy as a strict disciplinarian would be a bit like describing Attila The Hun as a social misfit. Still, I had miraculously survived nearly seven months of hard time in her class without cracking. Of course my survival was due more to good luck than consistent exemplary behavior as evidenced by my most recent and narrowest escape.

During one of our high-scoring, lunchtime softball games, I had tagged Jimmy Sullivan, the class creep, out on a close play at home. Sullivan, objecting to both the call and the excessively firm tag, made a loud and tasteless remark concerning my family lineage, and I responded by suggesting he attempt a biologically difficult maneuver.

Apparently, Sister Mary Mummy had been made aware of Sullivan's comment, because when we returned to "The Hole" for afternoon classes a glass of water containing a glistening bar of Ivory soap was resting on his desk. Naturally Sullivan's attention was focused on the sudsy object during Sister Mary Mummy's lecture on the First Continental Congress.

An hour later, she abruptly ended the lecture and summoned Sullivan to the front of the room.

"Sure thing, Sister," he said. "You want me to clean the blackboard or something?"

"Not exactly," said Sister Mary Mummy.

"The erasers?" Sullivan wailed. "I'm very good with

erasers."

"Move it, Sullivan," shouted Sister Mary Mummy. "And bring the soap with you."

"What soap?"

"The soap on your desk," said Sister Mary Mummy, producing a new, cellophane-wrapped toothbrush from her desk drawer. "You know, the kind that, unlike your vocabulary, is 99 and 44/100ths per cent pure."

Before Sullivan suffered the brief but humiliating ordeal of having his teeth brushed with soap, Sister Mary Mummy asked him if he had anything to say.

"Yeah," said Sullivan, looking directly at me, "I was safe by a mile."

He didn't implicate me though, and I found myself on the verge of actually not hating him for the first time.

Then, less than a month before summer vacation, I took a major fall.

We had entered the classroom in our usual formation and Sister Mary Mummy began the first lesson of the day, Confiscation IA. Since it was near the end of the school year, her desk was a literal warehouse of confiscated contraband. Sister Mary Mummy is generally credited with being the human forerunner of the metal detectors that have become as much a part of air travel as lost baggage, and the vast assortment of illegal items crammed into the bowels of her wooden vault was testimony to her effectiveness.

She had more squirt guns, comic books, and Juicy Fruit than a Five and Ten, and enough yo-yos to qualify as a Duncan distributor. She had even seized a well-thumbed copy of "God's Little Acre" that Dudley Mack, despite the lurid cover illustration, had tried to pass off as a religious tract.

"Mr. Mack, Mr. Hoffman, and Mr. Shea," said Sister Mary Mummy.

"Present," we answered, automatically.

"Please come to the front of the room," said Sister

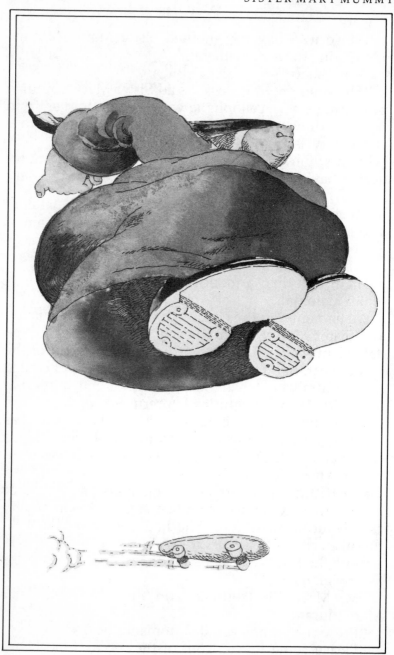

Mary Mummy.

I wasn't carrying anything on me, but I knew what she had found. Obviously, the others did too, but we tried to assume a puzzled air of innocence anyway. As we approached Sister Mary Mummy, though, I'm sure my expression conveyed the guilt and fear I was feeling inside.

"Mr. Mack," began Sister Mary Mummy, "please hand over the cigarette hidden between pages 243 and 244 of your English text."

Dudley returned to his desk and opened the book.

"How about that?" he said, extracting a flattened smoke. "I guess my father forgot his bookmark again."

"At least someone in your family opens your books," said Sister Mary Mummy, sarcastically. She disposed of the cigarette and cleared her throat.

"Now," she continued, "it has come to my attention that you three have been seen riding some silly contraption over on 34th Street recently."

We said the only thing we could think of; "Yes, S'ter."

"Are you aware," she thundered, "that leaving school property during school hours is not only frowned upon but that it is practically a felony?"

"Yes, S'ter."

"Good," she said. "At least you've learned *something* during your eight years at Our Lady of the Gulag."

The "silly contraption" she was referring to was a skateboard Dudley, Marty and I had jointly purchased and smuggled onto the school grounds. We kept it hidden in some bushes at the far end of the playground and on those days when Sister Mary Mummy was sentenced to cafeteria duty we would grab the board and sneak over to 34th Street.

"Who owns the thing?" asked Sister Mary Mummy.

"They do," said Dudley Mack quickly. Marty and I exchanged surprised looks because, until that moment, Dudley had claimed sole ownership because he had contributed twice as much toward its purchase as had Marty and I. Our respective shares, however, had come from precious allowances while Dudley's funds had come from the protection money he extorted from classmates.

"Well," said Sister Mary Mummy, "we'll discuss this further at the luncheon recess."

After the noon bell, she accompanied us to the skateboard's formerly secret resting place. Dudley crawled into the bushes and emerged moments later clutching the cause of our dismal predicament. He handed it over to Sister Mary Mummy.

"So this is a skateboard," she said.

"Sure is," said Dudley Mack.

"How does it work?" asked Sister Mary Mummy.

"You just climb aboard and sail," replied Dudley, striking a board-riding pose. "It ain't easy, Sister."

"It isn't?"

"No sir, S'ter, it sure ain't."

"Well," said Sister Mary Mummy, "I'll be the judge of that. Let's go."

"Where are we going?"

"34th Street," she said. "Where else?"

When we arrived at the smoothly-paved hill, Dudley demonstrated the handling characteristics of the board for Sister Mary Mummy. He executed a medium speed, graceful slalom between some imaginary pylons, and ended with a running dismount. Marty and I applauded his performance as he carried the board back up the hill.

Sister Mary Mummy tentatively placed her massive right foot on the skateboard and it immediately slithered out from under her and sped down the hill. Dudley ran after the riderless board and Marty whispered, "If she tries to ride that thing again, some orthopedic surgeon is going to need a lot of plaster."

Compared to today's technologically advanced skateboards, ours was incredibly primitive and dangerous. Non-skid fiberglass surfaces have replaced the slick

wood we used, and the tactile, sure-gripping polyure-
thane wheels on the current models are a vast improve-
ment over the tractionless metal wheels that propelled
our board. The new wheels, combined with a suspension system rivaling those found on many cars, make
riding a banked surface a thrilling experience instead of
a sure way of committing suicide. Additionally, the new
boards are more flexible than a politician discussing a
sensitive issue during an election year.

But it was just a plain wooden skateboard with slip-
pery metal wheels and no suspension to speak of that
Dudley Mack retrieved for Sister Mary Mummy on 34th
Street that day.

Her second attempt was moderately successful. She
even kept her balance while the board rolled over a man-
hole cover.

"Maybe we should call it a day, S'ter," suggested Marty
Shea.

"Nonsense," said Sister Mary Mummy, preparing to
mount the skateboard again. "This is too much fun."

On her third ride, she almost lost control at the halfway
point, but instead of abandoning ship she hung on and
regained her balance. Then she astounded us by doing a
series of 180 degree turns in rapid succession, a maneuver that had thus far eluded us.

"This is the last ride," Sister Mary Mummy announced
a few minutes later.

After picking up speed she went into a deep crouch on
the front edge of the board and executed the impossible:
a nose wheelie! She turned and waved at us as she straight-
ened up, but we were too stunned by her maneuver to
return the greeting. We were also stunned by the sight of
a car that had just backed out of the driveway directly
into Sister Mary Mummy's path.

Understandably, the driver panicked and stalled when
he saw the nun speeding toward him. So did Dudley
Mack.

"Oh, no," cried Dudley, "she's going to wreck a new Corvette."

Only a miracle could save Sister Mary Mummy and that's exactly what she had up her billowing habit sleeve. When she was just a few feet from the side of the convertible, she leaped high into the air and soared over the cowering driver as the passengerless skateboard disappeared under the vehicle. Because our vision was blocked by the Corvette we couldn't see what happened next, but somehow Sister Mary Mummy was reunited with the skateboard. She then made a high-speed, 90-degree turn into an upward sloping driveway, skidding to a halt only inches from the garage door.

And with that, the miracle of 34th Street was history.

As we walked back toward Our Lady of the Gulag, Sister Mary Mummy, the Catholic kamikaze, was strangely silent.

"Uh, are you going to keep the skateboard, S'ter?" Dudley Mack finally stammered.

"Yes, Mr. Mack," Sister Mary Mummy replied, "I am. But you may claim it on the last day of school."

Dudley looked especially pained when, after a long pause, she softly added, "Maybe..."   ❧

XIII

THE LORD'S SPRAYER

UDLEY MACK was in a foul mood.

"He looks like a bull elephant with a three-day migraine," whispered Marty Shea.

"Yeah," I agreed, "he hasn't been this bad since the Mickey Mouse club rejected his application for membership."

"What's wrong, Dud?" Marty ventured.

"What's *wrong*?" Dudley Mack thundered, "Did you say, 'what's *wrong*'?" The tone of his voice clearly indicated he felt Marty had taken complete and total leave of his senses. "Oh, nothing's wrong," he continued sarcastically, "nothing at all except that I watched the Colts' game on television yesterday."

"So?"

"Well," Dudley said with exaggerated patience, "the Colts only play on Sunday."

Marty and I glanced at each other and wondered where Dudley's convoluted logic was headed this time.

"And since yesterday was Sunday, this is Monday,

which means we are about to begin another five-day
stretch in *The Hole*." Dudley looked up at the row of win-
dows on Our Lady of the Gulag's third floor and Marty
and I involuntarily did the same. Sister Mary Mummy's
hulking figure was visible through the classroom win-
dows.

"Uh, Dudley," murmured Marty Shea, "I think she's
waving at us."

We awkwardly waved at the smiling nun on the third
floor and she began to turn away. Dudley was on the
verge of converting his wave into an obscene gesture
when Marty leaped at him and pinned his arms to his
side.

"Whaaaat?"

"Cool it, Dud," Marty hissed. "We got a couple of habits approaching from the starboard side."

"G'morning, S'ters," we chorused pleasantly a few
seconds later when Sister Mary Bigfoot and Sister Superior strolled past.

"That was a close one," sighed Dudley Mack when
they were out of range. "Thanks."

"Think nothing of it," replied Marty.

"Hi, guys!"

In our frantic efforts to shield Dudley from a certain
morals charge, we failed to notice that Jimmy Sullivan
was sneaking up on us.

"Jeeez," moaned Dudley, "this is all I need on a Monday morning."

As usual, Sullivan was completely oblivious to the undisguised dismay that greeted his sudden arrival in our
midst.

"I've been lookin' all over for you guys," said Sullivan.

"We ain't been all over," snarled Dudley Mack. "We've
been right here."

"I'm glad I finally found you because I've got some
incredible news."

"The state finally condemned your personality?"

"No," said Sullivan, "this is serious."

"Your pet bunny attempted suicide again?"

"C'mon, you guys," Sullivan whined in his most pathetic voice.

"OK," said Dudley Mack, "but it better be good."

"It is," Sullivan squealed, "it really is. Form a circle and I'll tell you all about it."

"We ain't a damn wagon train, Sullivan," said Dudley angrily. "Get on with it."

"Would you consider lining up in alphabetical order then?" Dudley wordlessly answered Sullivan's question by displaying an upraised fist.

"Uh, you know that my father is an instructor over at All Souls College?" Sullivan said quickly, not taking his eyes from Dudley's poised paw.

"Right. So?" All Souls was a Catholic women's college on the other side of town, and Sullivan's father was head of the Drama department.

"Well, last Saturday morning I went out to the college with my father, you know, to help out with a few of the sets and stuff, and when we were leaving, we drove past the swimming pool." Sullivan paused dramatically. "Guess who I saw?"

"Lloyd Bridges?"

"Esther Williams?"

"Captain Nemo?"

"Nope," said Sullivan. "I saw our dear friend and beloved teacher, Sister Mary Mummy."

"You're kidding?" said Marty Shea.

"I thought she already graduated from college," said Dudley Mack.

"She wasn't attending classes," said Sullivan, "she was *swimming*. In the swimming pool. I think Sister Mary Bigfoot and Sister Superior were with her."

"Wait a minute. Are you telling us that..."

"Right," Sullivan nodded solemnly. "In real, honest-to-God bathing suits."

Five minutes later Sullivan was still basking in the attention he was receiving from us when the class bell rang.

As we marched past Sister Mary Mummy into the classroom, Dudley Mack succumbed to the obvious temptation. "How was your weekend, S'ter?" he asked.

"Just fine, Mr. Mack," replied Sister Mary Mummy.

"Looks like you caught a few rays."

"As a matter of fact, I did," stammered the thoroughly puzzled nun as Dudley took his seat.

By mid-week, we had discovered that Sister Mary Mummy and several of her colleagues regularly piled into the convent's dilapidated station wagon on Saturday mornings and headed for the All Souls pool for a few hours in the sun. Armed with that extraordinary information, we prevailed upon Sullivan to find a way of getting us out there the following weekend.

"Good news, guys," he announced on Friday morning. "My dad has to go to the college tomorrow and he said we could come along. He's arranging for us to have the keys to the indoor gym so we can shoot some baskets while he's working." Sullivan lowered his voice conspiratorially. "The gym is right next to the pool."

The next morning, Sullivan's father handed us the key to the gym and said he'd pick us up later that afternoon. On the drive to All Souls he'd treated us to an in-depth analysis of Dwayne Hickman's acting ability and we had responded with a display of *real* acting by pretending we were interested. As soon as he drove off, we sprinted towards the pool.

Not counting the half-dozen dead leaves floating on the surface, it was empty.

"I knew it," Dudley said dejectedly. "They ain't coming."

"They'll be here," Sullivan said. "It's still early. Why don't we go in and shoot some baskets while we wait?"

"Hey, Jimmy," said Dudley Mack, "did I ever show

you my stuff shot?"

"Why no, Dud, you never have." If Sullivan was surprised by the fact that it was the first time Dudley had ever addressed him by his first name, it didn't show.

"Well if there ain't any nuns in that pool within an hour, you're gonna see it firsthand."

Since Dudley played basketball with all the finesse of a wrecking ball, barely twenty minutes had elapsed before Sullivan was stretched out on the floor contemplating his second bloody nose of the day.

"Hey, Dud," said the diplomatic Marty Shea, "I'm not entirely sure, but I seem to recall reading somewhere that a headlock is not a legal defensive maneuver in basketball."

"So sue me," laughed Dudley going in for a layup. As the ball dropped through the hoop, we heard the sound of a distant splash.

"They're here!"

Though the moment we were waiting for had arrived, we were suddenly reluctant to go out to the pool. All at once doing so seemed to be somehow sacrilegious. A brief debate about the wisdom of our scheme, however, resulted in a unanimous decision that the prospect of swimming nuns was just too good to pass up. We abandoned the basketball court and crept outside.

A narrow, dirt walkway bordered by a tall hedge stood between us and the pool.

"Over here," Sullivan whispered hoarsely. We followed him to a small opening in the hedge and peered through it. There were six nuns in attendance, and all were in the water except one. Sister Mary Mummy was reclining in a lounge chair not ten feet in front of us.

She was wearing a bright, white plastic swimming cap and was wrapped in an even brighter orange towel.

"Come on in, Sister," called one of the swimming nuns. "The water's perfect."

Sister Mary Mummy stood up and Dudley Mack

gasped.

"Look at her towel," he croaked.

The orange towel was emblazoned with a silhouetted image of a surfer and the printed legend, "Let's Go Trippin'."

Sister Mary Mummy dropped the garish, terrycloth beach towel, revealing a shapeless, single-piece black bathing suit that covered her from her neck to her knees. It easily dated back to the turn of the century.

"That thing must weigh an easy 40 pounds when it's wet," murmured Marty Shea.

"How come they're wearing bathin' caps?" asked Dudley. "I thought nuns shaved their heads."

"That's an old nun's tale," said Sullivan as we watched Sister Mary Mummy adjust her bathing cap strap and saunter towards the three-meter diving board. She effortlessly climbed the perpendicular aluminum ladder and assumed the classic diver's position on the fiberglass slab.

Displaying exquisitely graceful form, she approached the end of the flexible board, brought her arms up over her head, and drew her right knee up to her chest. The full impact of her weight caused the board to bend a full three feet before it recoiled and flung her skyward. At the peak of her ascent, Sister Mary Mummy went into a tuck position which she held for three-and-a-half revolutions. She split the water perfectly, leaving only a small circle of bubbling froth as testimony of her entrance.

"A three-and-a-half!" Dudley muttered with awe. "I can't believe it."

Sister Mary Mummy climbed out of the pool and mounted the ladder a second time. A veritable waterfall cascaded from the coarse folds of her suit. Her second approach mirrored the first, but instead of tucking when airborne, she executed a single front flip in the layout position and then added a half-twist. Her back was towards us as she plummeted towards the water. Just before impact, she leaned back and clasped her arms around her right knee. The force of her entry seemed to draw every drop of the chlorinated water in after her. Then suddenly and without warning, a huge geyser exploded towards the sky. The solid sheet of water rose higher and higher until it was at least 30 feet over our heads...directly over our heads.

Seconds later, Dudley, Marty, Sullivan and I were hit with every last drop. Drenched and shaken, we were back in the gym before Sister Mary Mummy surfaced.

"She *couldn't* have known we were there," said Dudley Mack. "No way."

"I tell you she did it on purpose," protested Marty Shea.

"Marty's right," said Sullivan. "It was too perfect to be an accident."

But we never really knew for sure because Sister Mary Mummy never mentioned anything about a well-aimed column of water and we, of course, never got around to asking her.   ~

XIV

ONE FLEW OVER THE CROSSBAR BEST

ARE YOU *SURE* this isn't against some Commandment or something?" whispered Jimmy Sullivan.

"For the last time," Marty Shea said patiently, "we aren't doing anything wrong."

"I can't believe it," mumbled Dudley Mack. "I mean, I've never been on Church property this long without breakin' *some* kinda rule."

"Those things happen," I said.

"Maybe," replied Dudley, "but it just ain't natural."

He was right of course. Our loitering presence on Our Lady of the Gulag's convent steps that Saturday morning was about as natural as a mail-order toupee', especially since we had come voluntarily and not under subpoena.

A pact allowing a graceful abandonment of our mission surely could have been formed if just two, or perhaps three, foolish souls had made the journey to the forbidding nunnery. With four of us in attendance, however, escape, even if mutually desirable, seemed somehow out of the question. So it was with a collective case of gut-wrenching nervousness that we waited.

"Look," said Marty Shea finally, "we agreed to do this together. Right?"

We nodded in silent unanimous affirmation.

"And the worst she can do is turn us down, right?"

"He's got a point, guys," said Sullivan softly.

"Then it's settled," said Marty. "Sullivan, you do the talking and we'll be right behind you."

"Yeah," said Dudley Mack, shoving the bewildered Sullivan towards the convent door, "we'll be waitin' in those bushes across the street."

We scrambled down the rickety steps in glorious, adrenalin-powered flight.

"*Halt!*"

The sharp command wrapped around us like a verbal lasso, instantly stopping our dash for safety.

"Uh, oh," muttered Marty Shea, "that's not Sullivan's voice."

"Where are you boys going?"

We turned and saw our ashen-faced comrade standing next to Sister Mary Mummy on the porch. The collar of his shirt was gathered in her massive right fist, his feet were dangling several inches off the floor, and his mouth was frozen in a grotesque definition of mute terror.

"I said, 'where are you boys going'?"

"The library."

"Church."

"Algebra practice." While not the most convincing liar at Our Lady of the Gulag, Dudley certainly scored points for originality.

"I see," smirked Sister Mary Mummy. "And you, Mr. Sullivan? Where are you going?"

"Nowhere, S'ter, absolutely nowhere," wailed Sullivan. "And I promise never to go there again."

Smooth-talking Marty Shea finally took the first step toward extricating us from our, ah, situation.

"Good morning, Sister," he said brightly, as if he was a detached observer rather than a principal player in the scene. "We came to see Sister Superior. We're interested in doing an extracurricular project and we need her permission.

"Well why didn't you say so in the first place?" said Sister Mary Mummy, releasing her grip on Sullivan. "Come in."

"Maybe we should come back some other time," said Dudley Mack. "In case she's busy prayin' or somethin'."

"Nonsense," replied Sister Mary Mummy. "She's in the recreation room getting whipped by Sister Mary Bigfoot." Noticing our looks of amusement, she added, "They play ping-pong every Saturday morning."

"Oh."

She then ushered us into the murky and mysterious confines of the convent.

"Nice place you've got here, S'ter," said Marty Shea glancing around the spartanly-furnished front room.

"Thank you, Mr. Shea," said Sister Mary Mummy. "Several of the Sisters wanted Danish Modern, but we finally decided on Early Religion." She picked up several issues of *The Catholic Digest* someone had left lying on the deacon's bench and tossed them aside. "Have a seat," she said. "I'll tell Sister Superior she has visitors."

We soon discovered that unless you've taken your final vows and have been fitted for a habit, it's absolutely impossible to make yourself comfortable in a convent. For the first time in my life, I found myself longing for a dental appointment.

Mercifully, Sister Mary Mummy reappeared a few minutes later and we practically sprinted after her as she escorted us to the convent's recreation room. Sure enough, Sister Superior, Our Lady of the Gulag's principal, was playing ping-pong with Sister Mary Bigfoot, the fourth-grade teacher.

"I'll be right with you," called Sister Superior from

across the sagging net of the ancient table.

Sister Mary Bigfoot was poised to serve. She slashed viciously at the ball, producing a looping serve whose backspin was plainly audible. The ball landed on Sister Superior's backhand side, and she gamely lunged at the rapidly retreating sphere, but missed it completely.

"That's it," said Sister Mary Bigfoot triumphantly, "21-4."

"Good game," muttered an obviously dejected Sister Superior. "If the devil was as wicked as your serve, we'd have to go on overtime."

Sister Mary Bigfoot laughed and left the room.

"Now, what can I do for you boys?"

"Well, Sister," said Marty Shea, continuing his role as spokesman, "we came to ask you about the vacant lot behind the convent there."

"Ah, yes" interrupted Sister Mary Mummy, "the 'Holy Land'."

"The *what*?"

"'The Holy Land'," said Sister Mary Mummy. "I believe that is how some of our students refer to our little piece of unused real estate. Am I right?"

"Now that you mention it, I think I have heard it called that," blurted Dudley Mack, the originator of the term.

"Anyway," continued Marty, "we'd like to convert the lot into a temporary athletic field so we can practice pole vaulting."

Sister Superior's hard-eyed stare unnerved Marty, but he pressed on. "We already talked to the Monsignor and he said itwasallrightwithhimifitwasallrightwithyou."

"What a splendid idea," said Sister Mary Mummy. "Inarticulately presented, but splendid."

"We already got a pole," chimed in Sullivan, "and Marty's dad is building us a pair of adjustable standards. All we need is a place to build a runway and a pit."

Sister Mary Mummy appeared not to have heard him. "You know, I once saw the great Cornelius Warmerdam vault in person. I swear, he was smoother than a used-car salesman's delivery," she said. "Of course I never got a chance to see the Reverend Bob Richards, but I heard he was something too."

"*Reverend* Bob Richards?" said Sister Superior.

"Certainly," replied Sister Mary Mummy. "Pole vaulting is nondenominational, Sister. Most sports are, you know."

"Bingo isn't," said Sister Superior testily, "and besides that's not what I meant. It just seems strange for a man of the cloth to engage in such pursuits, lofty though they may be."

"It made his congregation look up to him though, Sister."

"In a literal sense I suppose you're right."

"Sold a whole bunch of *Wheaties*, too," ventured Jimmy Sullivan.

Even with Sister Mary Mummy on our side of the argument for a change, it took us a half hour to convince Sister Superior that no convent is complete without pole vaulting facilities.

Despite Dudley's economically sound, but totally inappropriate suggestion that such an addition might increase the convent's resale price, she finally gave the project her blessing.

"But," cautioned Sister Superior, "I am making you fully responsible, Sister. Watch over your flakes carefully."

"Thank you, Sister," said Sister Mary Mummy, "but don't you mean *flock*?"

"Nope," said Sister Superior firmly.

Exactly one week later, everything was ready. The hard-packed runway began near the walnut tree next to the rectory fence, and the sawdust-filled landing pit was nestled against the convent's well-tended vegetable garden. The standards were in place, and we had even talked Sister Superior into letting us keep our 16-foot fi-

berglass vaulting pole in the basement of the convent.

Sister Mary Mummy had personally constructed the vitally important "box"; a triangular, aluminum-surfaced sloping hole in which the tip of the pole is planted and the vaulter's horizontal motion is converted into vertical flight.

"OK," said Sister Mary Mummy, "all systems are go. Who's jumping first?"

"We took a vote, S'ter," said Marty Shea, "and we unanimously agreed that you should be first."

Though obviously touched by our gesture, Sister Mary Mummy gracefully declined.

"In that case," said Dudley. "Sullivan'll go first and if he don't break his scrawny neck, I'll try it. You other guys can jump in alphabetical order."

"How high?" Sister Mary Mummy asked Sullivan.

"Four feet, eight-and-three-quarter inches," he replied without hesitation.

"That's not a pole vault," said Sister Mary Mummy disgustedly. "That barely qualifies as a high jump."

"But it's my lucky number," murmured Sullivan.

She set the crossbar at seven feet even and Sullivan dragged the pole to the top of the runway. After disentangling it from the low-hanging limbs of the walnut tree, he turned and sprinted mincingly toward the pit. Undoubtedly the nuns' entire vegetable garden was planted in less time than it took Sullivan to plant the pole. His aborted effort ended up looking more like a pratfall than a pole vault.

Since Sullivan didn't break his neck, Dudley Mack grabbed the pole and marched up the runway. Astoundingly, his form was even worse than Sullivan's and he knocked the crossbar off the standards with his forehead.

Marty and I both had some vaulting experience, and we cleared seven feet easily despite the fact that neither of us had enough speed or weight to make the pole bend properly.

Without comment, Sister Mary Mummy lowered the bar to three-and-a-half feet for Sullivan's next attempt, but again he missed badly.

Then, with a look of fierce determination, Dudley lumbered down the runway like a crazed water buffalo. He missed the box completely and landed face down in the mountain of fresh sawdust.

Spewing invectives and sawdust with equal ferocity, he grabbed a sharp stone and began hacking at the pole.

"Hey! What are you doing?" screamed Marty.

"I'm going to remove my four feet of the pole," Dudley replied calmly. "And then I'm going to beat you guys over the head with it for talking me into investing my hard-earned dough in this thing." Earned was Dudley's peculiar euphemism for "stolen."

"That's crazy!" yelled Marty, who was becoming slightly hysterical.

"Wrong," shouted Dudley through sawdust-coated teeth. He pointed at the gently swaying crossbar. "*That's* crazy!"

"Cool it!" yelled Sister Mary Mummy, and we did. "Now," she said soothingly, "I'm not an expert or anything, but I think I spotted some basic flaws in your approach to vaulting. Being deliberate isn't quite enough, Mr. Sullivan, nor is strength all that matters, Mr. Mack." Then she deflated Marty and I. "Luck isn't everything either."

She picked up the pole and began to walk toward the distant walnut tree. "How high does that thing go?" she called over her shoulder.

"Uh, 20 feet, S'ter," said Marty.

"Well, crank 'er up."

"But the world's record is only..."

"Just get that crossbar up there and stand back," she ordered.

While Dudley and Marty struggled to raise the crossbar, Sullivan and I watched Sister Mary Mummy perform her pre-jump ritual.

"Look," said Sullivan excitedly as she bent down to tie her shoes, "she's wearing *spikes!*"

After attaining proper lace tensions, Sister Mary Mummy reached down, grabbed a handful of loose dirt and began rubbing it vigorously into the palms of her hands. Dudley and Marty successfully raised the bar to its position 20 feet above the ground.

"Ready?" called Sister Mary Mummy.

"Ready, S'ter."

She paused briefly, firmed her grip on the pole and took off. As she thundered down the runway like some exotic, horseless Black Knight looking for Sir Lancelot, Dudley Mack mentioned something about her being indicted by the F.A.A. for failing to file a flight plan if she cleared the bar.

Then the tip of the pole was in the aluminum-lined box and Sister Mary Mummy's spiked shoes were pointing heavenward. The pole bowed like an over-ripe sapling and, for a brief instant, Sister Mary Mummy's long, black veil rested on the ground. Suddenly, the pole unwound and she was violently catapulted toward the crossbar. She went into a classic vaulter's handstand and twisted her body 180°. As her feet, then her legs, rose above the metal crossbar, she released her grip on the pole and jackknifed but her momentum carried her higher still. As she hung a good six inches over the crossbar, I thought I saw a flash of fear in her eyes.

"She actually did it!" cried Dudley Mack, falling to his knees.

Marty caught the pole, and the sawdust pit caught Sister Mary Mummy.

"Jumping with metal poles was more of a challenge," was all she said after climbing out of the pit.

We were still speechless when Sister Superior wandered out to inspect the vaulting apparatus a few minutes later.

"Sister," she said, as she approached us, "you're covered with sawdust. You know that's a flagrant violation of Our Lady of the Gulag's habit code."

"Sorry," said Sister Mary Mummy with a sly wink in our direction. "It won't happen again."

And to this day, it hasn't. You can look it up.   ∾

XV

LET US PLAY

WHAT A BEAUTIFUL DAY," said Marty Shea.
"Sure is," I agreed. "Isn't it a beautiful day, Dud?"

Dudley Mack, who was busy carving his name in the middle slat of the park bench upon which the three of us were sprawled, interrupted his labor and stared at me with undisguised contempt. After a moment, he muttered something about my family lineage and returned to the task of defiling public property with the pearl-handled pocket knife he had "borrowed" from McCall's drugstore less than an hour before.

Dudley Mack was a cretinous misanthrope who rarely saw beauty in anything that couldn't be classified as a weapon, but Marty and I hung out with him anyway. Our fear/hate relationship with Dudley had begun several years earlier on the first day of our first year at Our Lady of the Gulag. I clearly remember that distant September morning when Dudley approached us in the schoolyard. At first we thought he was the custodian.

That sounds funny now, but it was an easy mistake to make. After all, not that many first-graders need a shave.

"You two," Dudley bellowed, "get your butts over here!"

We hastily complied with his request.

"What grade are you guys in?"

"First grade, sir."

"Me too," announced the overgrown seven-year-old.

Marty and I exchanged terrified looks as Dudley slowly circled us. He was obviously looking us over very carefully, but we had no idea why. Finally, Dudley ended the inspection.

"Well, I guess this is your lucky day," he said, "because I have decided that you two are going to be my best friends until we get out of this dump."

"But...," said Marty Shea.

"I don't like to do stuff by myself so..."

"...but...," I said.

"...so the three of us will hang out together after school and on weekends and stuff."

Marty and I decided to accept Dudley's offer of friendship because neither of us had a death wish, nor did we have enough ready cash to finance a trip out of the country. Over the years, however, we actually developed a mild case of respect for the guy although we stopped far short of actually liking him. Part of the reason for this was that we were never quite sure whether or not his frequent threats to cut off our ears and mail them to Mary Margaret Delicate were serious.

I had closed my eyes and was thinking about how tough life would be without ears when Marty Shea suddenly leaped to his feet. "We've been cooped up in a lousy classroom all week," he shouted, "and now we have a whole day of freedom."

"A whole *beautiful* day of freedom," corrected Dudley Mack in a tone of voice best described as reeking with sarcasm.

"So how come we're bored out of our skulls?"

"What is this," asked Dudley, "a quiz?"

We were trying to come up with an answer to Marty's question when Mary Margaret Delicate showed up. She was wearing an immaculate white blouse and a pair of white shorts whose creases were undoubtedly sharper than the blade of Dudley's knife. Brilliant white tennis shoes on her feet and a white satin ribbon in her hair completed the outfit. On the whole, Mary Margaret's personal appearance was testimony to the fact that she tended to view the slightest scuff, soil, or wrinkle in much the same way the average person tends to view leprosy.

"Hello, boys," she said brightly. "I...oh, I didn't know *he* was with you."

She meant Dudley of course. He had just emerged from a nearby clump of bushes, the latest site of one of his frequent "pit stops."

"Howdy, M.M.," said Dudley. "You off to your weekly mud fight?"

Mary Margaret totally ignored him, a fact that neither upset nor surprised anyone, least of all Dudley Mack. Mary Margaret hadn't said a single word to him in over five years; not since the day she told him he could go straight to "h-e-double toothpicks" right after he forced her to look at his report card, thereby causing her to throw up in front of the entire third-grade class.

"Where *are* you going?" asked Marty Shea.

"Actually, I'm on my way to the tennis courts," replied Mary Margaret. "Maureen Connolly is going to conduct a clinic. Free."

"Who the hell is Marlene Crowley?" asked Dudley.

"Tell him her name is Maureen Connolly and that she is only the best tennis player in the entire world," said Mary Margaret angrily. She began walking toward the courts. "By the way," she called over her shoulder, "Sister will be there."

140

Her parting words momentarily stunned us. Sister
Mary Mummy, the iron-fisted disciplinarian, the scourge
of Our Lady of the Gulag, the Babe Didrickson of Catholicism, and the personal nemesis of Dudley Mack, would
be at the tennis courts in person! On a Saturday morning!

Dudley was elated. *"Now* we got ourselves somethin'
to do," he said. "Tennis, anyone?"

The wicked gleam in his eyes told us he had something
unspeakable in mind so we tried to talk him out of attending the tennis clinic, but to no avail.

"She can't do nothin' to us on neutral turf," he reasoned.

A few minutes later we were mingling with the crowd
that was gathering at the tennis courts in the park. Temporary bleachers had been erected next to the chain link
fence that surrounded the four courts, and several dozen
folding chairs had been set up on the court adjacent to
the one on which the clinic would be held. We were
checking things out and keeping a sharp lookout for Sister Mary Mummy when we heard a familiar voice. The
sound made us cringe.

"Guys! Hey, guys! Over here!"

Out of the corner of my eye I could see Jimmy Sullivan
frantically waving at us from the bleachers. Like Mary
Margaret Delicate, he too, was clad in white.

"If that creep comes within 10 feet of me, I swear I'll
carve my name in his forehead," said Dudley Mack.

Less than 30 seconds later, Sullivan was standing next
to Dudley, grinning like an idiot.

"Hi, Dud. Hi guys," he said cheerfully. Sullivan was
always cheerful, friendly and full of good humor. And
those were just three of the reasons we hated him.

"I didn't know you liked tennis, Dud," continued Sullivan, oblivious, as usual, to our lack of enthusiasm at
finding ourselves once again in his singularly irritating
company.

"I don't," said Dudley. "In fact, I hate tennis. It's a

sissy game."

"Oh no it's not," whined Sullivan. "I play all the time."

"I rest my case," said Dudley triumphantly.

Sullivan started to say something else, but thought better of it and fell silent.

"Hey, there she is," yelled Marty Shea.

Sure enough, Sister Mary Mummy was slowly making her way through the crowd on the other side of the court.

"You know, from a distance she looks a little like Mt. McKinley," said Marty.

In spite of the distance between us and the noise of the crowd, we could clearly hear the distinctive, but oh-so-familiar clicking of Sister Mary Mummy's rosary beads as she climbed over the wooden bleachers.

"Say, isn't that Mary Margaret Delicate with the Sister?" asked Sullivan. Sullivan was infatuated with Mary Margaret, but even *she* had the good sense to find him repulsive. Not nearly as repulsive as she found Dudley, of course, but repulsive just the same.

"Who else?" muttered Marty Shea.

"I think she really likes me," said Sullivan, "if you know what I mean."

"I'm sure she does," said Marty. "And the Pope's Jewish."

Sister Mary Mummy finally located an acceptable seat, and her ubiquitous sidekick quickly sat down next to her. From our vantage point, the sight of Mary Margaret's white outfit against Sister Mary Mummy's black habit gave one the unmistakable impression of a giant domino with a solitary pip.

Dudley, Marty and I were still trying to figure out how to get rid of Sullivan without resorting to a capital crime when Maureen Connolly strode onto the court to an enthusiastic, mostly dignified round of applause. The greeting would have been *totally* dignified had Sister Mary Mummy restrained herself from rising to her feet and screaming "Little Mo, Little Mo" over and over.

The tennis player, as well as the majority of the spectators, stared at the screaming, wildly applauding nun in bewilderment. Sister Mary Mummy eventually realized that all eyes were upon her, and she sat down, obviously embarrassed. Mary Margaret Delicate, who had a horrified look plastered on her face which was now whiter than her apparel, appeared to be terminally mortified.

The brief spectacle delighted Dudley as much as it dismayed Mary Margaret, and it gave him a new respect for Sister Mary Mummy.

"I've disrupted a lot of classrooms in my time," he whispered, "but I've never disrupted a *public* gathering."

Meanwhile, Maureen Connolly composed herself, leaned her tennis racquets against the net, and began to address the crowd in a loud, clear voice. Sullivan was listening with rapt attention, but Marty, Dudley, and I were busy reading the mimeographed biography of the player that had been handed out earlier.

I knew practically nothing about tennis and absolutely nothing about Maureen Connolly. And although I didn't fully understand the significance of her accomplishments, which, according to the biography, included winning the singles title at Forest Hills and Wimbledon three times in a row each, and being the first woman to win the Grand Slam, all while still in her teens, they certainly sounded impressive enough.

I was in the midst of reading about the 1954 horseback riding accident that had forced her retirement from active competition at the age of 19 when Dudley stuck his copy of the biography in my face and stabbed at it with his humongous forefinger.

"What's that word?" he asked.

"Uh, Dud, that word is 'welcome'." Dudley and the written word enjoyed only a nodding acquaintance. He recognized most of the letters in the alphabet, but combinations of four or more of them totally threw him.

Having completed her introductory remarks, Little Mo

began hitting tennis balls with a local club pro, an old guy in his 20's. Despite the fact that she was simultaneously hitting the ball and explaining the mechanics of the strokes to several hundred people, the fuzzy, white spheres were leaping off her racquet strings with a velocity that was totally disproportionate to the amount of effort she seemed to be expending. Before long, her partner was dripping sweat and panting heavily, but Little Mo still looked crisp and cool. She ended the groundstroke demonstration by casually drilling a backhand screamer down the line, just out of the reach of the frantic stretch of the pro while holding a large bucket of balls in her left hand.

After running through the basics of serving and volleying, Little Mo, who had thoroughly captivated the assembled, with the possible and not too surprising exception of one Dudley L. Mack, asked her assisant to retrieve the dozens of tennis balls that were scattered around. She then invited all those who had brought racquets to the clinic to join her on the court.

"Alright!" shouted Sister Mary Mummy, withdrawing a tennis racquet from somewhere deep within the bountiful folds of her habit with a flourish that surely would have made D'Artagnan envious.

Two dozen or so people who had initially accepted Little Mo's invitation froze in their tracks when they saw the nun scrambling out of the bleachers. By the time Sister Mary Mummy had made her way to the player's side, the others had melted back into the crowd.

Little Mo pleaded with them to join her but not one of them stepped forward.

"Well, Sister," she finally sighed, "I guess it's just you and me."

"I've always believed in miracles," said Sister Mary Mummy. "It's part of my job, you know. I never dreamed I would actually experience one though, but here I am on a tennis court with Little Mo!"

Little Mo, a rather small woman, looked extremely uncomfortable standing next to the towering nun. She had met stiffer challenges before, but probably none taller. "Have you played much tennis, Sister?"

"I used to," replied Sister Mary Mummy, "but not recently. I had to give up my country club membership when I took my vow of poverty." The small joke got a small laugh from the large crowd.

"Vow of poverty?" said Little Mo. "I thought only amateur athletes had to take that one. Anyway, perhaps you wouldn't mind hitting a few with me."

"Another miracle," screeched Sister Mary Mummy. "I can't stand it!"

With that, she leaped over the net, briefly exposing a pair of new tennis shoes in the process, and positioned herself behind the baseline. "Ready when you are, Champ," she called.

Dudley was practically beside himself with excitement. "C'mon, S'ter," he yelled, "cream her!"

"Uh, Dud, I really don't think it's proper to yell during a tennis match," said Marty.

"You puttin' me on?"

"Nope."

"Well, can I throw things?"

"Afraid not."

"What *can* I do?"

"Hold your breath and pretend you're in church."

"But I always throw things in church."

While Marty was giving Dudley a crash course in proper spectatorial behavior, Sister Mary Mummy and Little Mo were trading groundstrokes that were becoming increasingly more vicious. Though it had been several years since Little Mo's career-ending accident, she was showing that she could still move around the court pretty well. And although she was somewhat hampered by her attire, Sister Mary Mummy was proving that she was no slouch when it came to mobility either.

Following a particularly long and exciting rally that
ended when Little Mo netted a cross-court forehand
drive, Sister Mary Mummy brazenly suggested that they
play an abbreviated two-games-out-of-three match. Little Mo agreed to the nun's proposal and motioned for her
to take the first serve.

After taking a few practice serves, in which she displayed a form that will most likely never appear in an
instruction manual, Sister Mary Mummy indicated that
she was ready.

Her first offering streaked across the net and caught
the back edge of the service line. Ace!

"Nice serve," said Little Mo graciously.

Sister Mary Mummy followed her next serve in to the
net and put away Little Mo's lob return with a magnificent, leaping, back-pedaling overhead. Someone standing behind me excitedly whispered that her style was
eerily reminiscent of the legendary Suzanne Lenglen's.

"She hits me with a ruler almost every day," Dudley
proudly informed the startled bystander.

The next two points were over almost before they began as Little Mo unaccountably committed consecutive
unforced backhand errors. Game One to Sister Mary
Mummy.

Though not a particularly strong server or volleyer
even when she was at her competitive peak, Little Mo
dominated Game Two with a tremendous combination
of well-placed services, deep drives to the corners, and
at least two volleys that were, well, miraculous. I began
to suspect that she may have performed an act of charity
in allowing Sister Mary Mummy to take the first game.

With the game score tied, Sister Mary Mummy suddenly did something I had never seen her do before: she
folded like a napkin.

After quickly falling behind love-40 in Game Three,
she drilled another overhead for a winner and then executed a brilliant drop shot after keeping Little Mo pinned

to the baseline for several shots. Sister Mary Mummy was now just one point away from getting even.

As she tossed the ball to serve at 30-40, Dudley shouted, "C'mon, Sister, you can do it! Knock it down her throat!"

A middle-aged woman standing next to us promptly fainted, apparently overcome by Dudley's spectacular breach of tennis etiquette. Meanwhile, Marty, Sullivan and I desperately tried to pretend we didn't know the loud-mouthed vulgarian who was responsible.

Sister Mary Mummy caught the service toss, looked directly at us, and *smiled*. She gently placed her forefinger against her pursed lips in the universal gesture requesting silence, and although even to this day I can't be sure, it looked like she actually winked at us.

Turning back to the task at hand, she tossed the ball skyward, reached up, and blasted it a good six feet past the service line. It was her first fault of the day, not counting, of course, the scene she had caused earlier. Her second serve was a screaming blur that hit the net tape with a loud 'crack' and dropped back onto her side of the court. Sister Mary Mummy had double faulted away her chance to pull even. The match was over. Final score: Little Mo, 2; Sister Mary Mummy, 1.

Several weeks later, Dudley approached Sister Mary Mummy after school one day.

"You remember when you played tennis against Marilee Crabtree?" he asked.

"If you mean Maureen Connolly," replied Sister Mary Mummy, "I remember it quite well."

"Well, uh, uh," stammered Dudley, "did you, uh, did you throw that match, S'ter?"

"Did I *what*?"

"You know," said Dudley, "did you lose on purpose?"

"Mr. Mack," replied Sister Mary Mummy, her chiseled features softened by a beatific smile, "if you don't learn anything else from me, and with your study habits that seems to be almost a certainty, I want you to learn one thing, and I don't ever want you to forget it. Barring an act of God, there was no way in heaven I could have beaten Little Mo. Nobody beats the best."   ⌇

XVI

THE HOLY ROMAN UMPIRE

HE SILENCE in the damp little room that functioned as Our Lady of the Gulag's candle closet and locker room was broken only by the metronomic sound of Dudley Mack's massive right fist slamming into the well-oiled, leather pocket of his pitcher's mitt.

A few feet away, Jimmy Sullivan, our fiesty shortstop, was gracefully plucking imaginary grounders off the bare concrete floor and firing phantom strikes to first baseman "Fat" Chance, who was studiously ignoring Sullivan's antics.

I, meanwhile, was thoroughly engrossed in my usual pre-game ritual of stuffing Kleenex deep into my flimsy catcher's mitt to provide additional protection against Dudley Mack's blister-producing fastball.

"Look at Sullivan," whispered Marty Shea, as another invisible runner fell victim to the shortstop's arm. "He even closes his eyes when he's pretending."

"Yeah," I replied, "but at least he's consistent. He

closes his eyes when he bats too."

"Hey," Marty said, "do you remember the time he actually hit the ball and then ran the wrong way?"

"Right. He was the first player in history to turn an easy triple into a close single."

"I'll never forget the look on the first baseman's face when ol' Sullivan slid into the bag waving the spikes in the guy's face."

A few minutes later Marty spoke again. "You nervous?" he asked.

"Sure I am," I said. "I've never played in a championship game before. Do you think we have a chance to win?"

"What do you mean? We're undefeated aren't we? We have a great coach, we have Dudley Mack's fireballs, and we have a lot of desire. O.K., maybe we do have a shortstop who's capable of making three errors walking from the dugout to the on-deck circle, but no team's perfect, not even the Yankees."

"I guess you're right," I said.

"We're gonna get massacred," said Marty Shea solemnly. "We have about as much of a chance as a snowball in H-E-double toothpicks."

"I'm not quite that confident." I said.

A lot of people were calling the Our Lady of the Gulag Crimson Tide a miracle team because of our unprecedented seven-game winning streak. Never before in the long and colorful history of that institution had any of its athletic teams won even two games in a row, much less a shot at the league championship. Of course, we owed our streak to Dudley Mack's right arm and more good luck than any team has a right to expect. After dropping our opening game to St. John the Other Baptist, we were behind in our second outing 7-0 when the entire St. Louis School team was placed on academic suspension in the middle of the third inning. We owed our second victory to another forfeit that occurred when the St. Stephen squad unanimously voted to stay after school and clean the blackboards rather than face Dudley's pitching. We won our next five narrowly, but legitimately, and in a few hours we would take the field against Our Lady of Perpetual Angst, with the league championship going to the winner.

Suddenly Coach Inconsulata entered the locker room. As usual his presence snapped us into immediate lethargy. Coach Inconsulata was a rough-edged, marginally-intelligent man, who had an incredible grasp of the intracacies of the game, but was wholly incapable of transmitting even the tiniest shred of his knowledge to his players. Though he had briefly played in the majors years before, he possessed a monumental lack of coordination.

"Men," he said, attempting to clap his hands together and failing miserably, "I have a little suprise for you."

"Our Lady of Perpetual Angst chickened out?" someone asked hopefully.

"No, nothing like that," said Coach Inconsulata. "Monsignor Munchkin has consented to stop by and dispense a few words of encouragement."

"Thank you, Coach Inconsulata," said Monsignor Munchkin. "Boys, I will keep this very short." He smiled wanly as he waited for the applause to subside so he could continue.

"Thank you, Coach Inconsulata," he repeated before abruptly crumbling the index card he was reading and tossing it over his shoulder. "Uh, uh, oh yes. Here we are." He cleared his throat and began to read from another card. "I want to say that everyone at Our Lady of the Gulag is proud of the tremendous job you boys have done and, as you know, our trophy case always has room for one more. Ha! Ha!" Monsignor Munchkin paused and pretended not to notice the absence of laughter. "But," he said dramatically, "if you should happen to lose, don't be ashamed. After all, no one really expects you to win anyway."

"OK, Monsignor," yelled Coach Inconsulata, "We'll see you at the game."

"I'm, uh, I'm afraid not, Coach," mumbled Monsignor Munchkin. "I'm teeing off at two o'clock this afternoon."

Another round of applause greeted that announcement, and the nervous little priest left the locker room with a timid wave.

An hour later the team bus pulled into the parking lot at Elysian Field, Our Lady of Perpetual Angst's home park.

"There she is, right on time," said Marty Shea.

Sure enough, Sister Mary Mummy, our unofficial mascot, official statistician, and sole fan, was standing near the chicken-wire backstop intently watching our opponents' batting practice.

The bus's squeaky brakes alerted her to our arrival, and she walked over as we disembarked from *The Yellow Peril.*

"Hello, boys," she said, hefting our equipment bag and carrying it towards the visitors' dugout. "I've been watching these guys, and they don't look all that tough. I figure their .768 team batting average is a fluke."

"Oh yeah?" said Marty Shea, as a wiry kid wearing number 19 belted a pitch over the distant centerfield fence. "Check out that little guy's power."

"Anyone can look good in batting practice," replied Sister Mary Mummy, "with the possible exception of Sullivan."

"Maybe," said Dudley Mack. "But he hit that thing one-handed."

Sister Mary Mummy dropped the equipment bag and consulted the roster on her clipboard. "Don't worry about him," she said. "He's third string."

Several months earlier, I had asked Sister Mary Mummy why she attended all of Our Lady of the Gulag's baseball games.

"I just love baseball," she said, "and since there aren't

any real teams around, I have to be content with watching you guys, pitiful though you may be."

Her remark came to mind as I watched my teammates struggle through infield practice. Of course the poor condition of the playing field contributed to our display of incompetence. It had more gouges and ruts than a back-country road after a long, hard winter, and the outfield grass was so high that outfielders appeared to be playing on their knees.

"Get with it, Shea," Sister Mary Mummy yelled after the normally steady third baseman let a slow grounder roll up his arm and over his shoulder into left field. "I could've handled that one barehanded with my eyes closed. You guys look like an outtake from a Keystone Cops movie."

When it became apparent that we weren't going to improve, Coach Inconsulata whistled us in from the field and began going over the starting lineup. A few minutes later, Our Lady of Perpetual Angst's coach approached our dugout. He looked grim.

"I've got some rather disturbing news," he said.

"What's wrong?" asked Coach Inconsulata.

"The umpire called in sick and we don't have a replacement."

"We're Number One!" screamed Dudley Mack, immediately grasping the fact that a forfeit was imminent.

"I'm afraid we'll have to forfeit," said the crestfallen coach.

"Gee, that's a real shame," lied Coach Inconsulata, "but we can't play without an umpire."

"Just a moment, gentlemen," interrupted Sister Mary Mummy. "You can't decide a league championship this way."

"Do you have any other ideas, Sister?" asked Our Lady of Perpetual Angst's coach.

"Certainly," replied Sister Mary Mummy. "I will serve as umpire."

"That's very generous of you, Sister," said Coach Inconsulata hurriedly, "but...but..."

"Are you questioning my qualifications, Coach Inconsulata?"

"No, of course not," he sputtered, "it's just that..."

"Can you be impartial, Sister?" asked the opposing coach.

Sister Mary Mummy fixed him with an icy glare. "Could Babe Ruth bounce 'em off the upper deck?"

"What about protection?" asked Coach Inconsulata.

"I'll take care of that," replied Sister Mary Mummy. She began to jog toward the parking lot.

"I'll be back in a minute."

Dudley and I went out in front of our dugout to warm up his pitching arm. He had thrown about a dozen scorchers when he stopped in mid-windup and stared disbelievingly past me.

"Oh, my God," he gasped. "Look at *that.*"

Sister Mary Mummy was trotting towards us wearing a hastily improvised umpire uniform that made her look like some kind of surrealistic executioner. A large, graffiti-covered seat cushion from *The Yellow Peril* was strapped to her chest, and her face was hidden behind the wire basket that was usually attached to the handlebars of the bicycle she rode to the games. She was also carrying a full-size broom in her right hand, and when she reached home plate, she began sweeping frantically. Almost immediately she raised a dust cloud straight out of "The Grapes of Wrath."

"Play ball!" she yelled when the dust finally settled.

The first four innings were scoreless and hitless and it was obvious that a pitcher's duel was in the making.

Our Lady of Perpetual Angst's pitcher wasn't anywhere near as fast as Dudley, but we just weren't making contact. Dudley, meanwhile, was superb, as always. He had given up only one foul ball while retiring the first 12 batters. And Sister Mary Mummy had, as expected, assumed a complete air of neutrality, confining her conversation to calling the balls and strikes.

In the top of the fifth I came to bat with one down and the bases empty. The count went to two balls and two strikes and I dug in for the next pitch. I was so sure that it would be a fast one down the middle that I made no attempt to get out of the way when the ball sailed in on me, slamming into my ribs. The pain was excruciating as I tossed my bat away and began to jog toward first base.

"Just a minute," called Sister Mary Mummy. "You can't take first. You let yourself get hit. The count is three balls and two strikes."

"But S'ter," I said, "I couldn't..."

"Batter up," she said.

Reluctantly, I retrieved my bat and took a pitch that missed the outside corner by a foot. Again I headed for first.

"Stike three!" yelled Sister Mary Mummy. "You're outta there."

"What!"

"You heard me," she said. "If your tail isn't on the bench within five seconds, you're out of the game."

I was sulking in the dugout when Dudley, the next batter, drove one out of the park. We were ahead 1-0 and the score stayed that way until the bottom of the ninth.

Dudley struck out the first two batters with ease and we were only a single out from the championship.

Kicking his left leg higher than a Radio City Rockette, Dudley sent the next pitch rocketing toward the plate. The ball was traveling so fast it looked smaller than a golf ball, but the batter stayed with it and unleashed a vicious swing that sent the pitch halfway to the state line. We were tied up and the prospect of extra innings loomed unpleasantly. Nine innings of catching Dudley Mack's fastball, the only pitch in his arsenal, was about all I could endure. My right hand already resembled a half-pound of ground chuck, and my ribs were still sore.

I was cataloging my ills when the next batter accidentally lined one down the left field line while trying to get away from an inside pitch.

"Fair ball!" screamed Sister Mary Mummy, throwing off her wire basket and hustling toward third. The ball and the runner arrived at approximately the same time, but she was right on top of the play.

"Safe!"

The winning run was on third and Our Lady of Perpetual Angst's weakest hitter was in the box.

"Strike!" The ball tore into my glove and set my hand on fire.

"Strike two!" The batter missed on a bunt attempt and the fire in my palm intensified.

The next pitch was in the dirt, but I managed to block it. I spun around and threw off my mask.

"Where's the ball?" I screamed.

Dudley Mack charged in from the mound to cover the plate, and Sister Mary Mummy was running backward to give me some room, but I still couldn't find the ball. Our Lady of Perpetual Angst's third base coach noticed my confusion and waved the runner home.

Then I saw the ball. It was under the hem of Sister Mary Mummy's habit. I dove toward her feet.

"Throw the damn ball," Dudley screamed as the runner bore down on him. "Sorry, S'ter," he muttered automatically.

I managed a weak underhanded toss in his direction and he met the sliding runner with a perfect tag.

"Safe!" yelled Sister Mary Mummy with the classic palms-down sweeping motion and absolutely no hesitation.

We, of course, protested the call that had cost us the league title, but, like all good umpires, Sister Mary Mummy declined to change her mind.

"When I officiate a ball game," she said, "many are called, but none are wrong."   ∿

XVII

RUN, HABIT, RUN

ARTY SHEA, Dudley Mack and I were lying on the infield grass near the finish line of La Bamba High's quarter-mile track speculating on whether or not Jimmy Sullivan would manage to lurch through the final half of his final lap. From our vantage point we could see that he was on the verge of packing it in, an observation that, in view of his well known reluctance to voluntarily confront the difficult, the challenging or the painful, led us to unanimously conclude that completion was out of the question.

Consequently, we were more than a little surprised when Sullivan, his chest heaving, his mouth opened wide to gulp the late afternoon air, and his pipestem arms flailing wildly about like those of a punchdrunk barroom brawler who's three sheets to the wind, rounded the last turn and wobbled rubber-legged and woozy into the home stretch. But even when faced with this totally uncharacteristic display of intestinal fortitude, we stubbornly clung to our collective conviction that he would never reach the finish line.

"Hey, Sullivan," yelled Dudley, "if you're plannin' to take off, you better do it now, you bozo, 'cuz you're almost outta runway." Then: "My granma' could outrun you with both legs tied behind her back."

Unaccountably, Sullivan responded to Dudley's lame insults with a sudden burst of speed that lasted a half dozen stumbling strides and carried him to within 10 yards or so of the finish. Then his tiny reservoir of reserve energy ran dry. Having fought the good fight, his legs suddenly gave up on him and he commenced the inevitable collapse. His momentum, however, carried him forward further still, until he finally belly-flopped onto the hard ground, bounced once or twice, and skidded to a halt at our feet.

"I'll be damned," yawned Marty, gazing down at the exhausted runner's prone figure. "He made it."

Sure enough, Sullivan's sweat-streaked brow was resting on the faint line of smeared chalk that meandered across the red cinders of the track.

"I'm dying," he groaned, rolling over onto his back and throwing a skinny forearm across his eyes. "I swear to God I am."

"Promises, promises," said Dudley as if he meant it, which he probably did. Although no one was particularly fond of Sullivan, Dudley sincerely detested him, a fact the monumentally annoying little guy was either unable or unwilling to grasp.

"That's a good joke, ol' buddy," Sullivan wheezed. "Thanks for trying to make my last minutes happy ones. I'll never forget it."

"I wasn't joking," snarled Dudley, "but if you thought that was funny, you gutless wonder, you'll probably get a real big kick outta havin' me plant my heels in your solar plexus, which is exactly what I aim to do in about five seconds."

"What a kidder," said Sullivan, embarking on a miraculous recovery from his brief, self-diagnosed brush with death. He struggled into a sitting position. "By the way," he said, "did you guys get my time?"

"Sure did," said Marty.

"How'd I do?"

"Well, let me put it this way: I wouldn't be in any big hurry to clear a space for my Olympic medals if I were you. You did a 4:18.3."

Sullivan swore mightily under his recently recaptured breath.

"Anything wrong?" asked Marty innocently.

"Plenty," responded Sullivan. "I wanted to break four minutes so bad I could taste it."

"Hey, I don't blame you. There's probably not more than six or seven people in the world who can't run an 880 in under four."

"There's more than that," said Sullivan defensively.

"I don't think so, Sully. You're in pretty select company."

&

Our presence at the deserted track was not the result of careful planning, but rather a combination of seemingly unrelated circumstances: the lack of somewhere better to hang out, and Dudley Mack's legendary nimble-fingeredness.

Earlier that afternoon we had been loitering at a downtown bus stop waiting for one of La Bamba's rolling smoke bombs to show up while reviewing the equally noxious double-feature we had just endured.

"If you ask me," Marty had said without being asked, " 'The Monster That Devoured Miami' took liberties well beyond those generally associated with film of that particular genre."

"What do you mean, Mart?" asked a baffled Sullivan.

"I mean," replied Marty with an exaggerated show of patience, "gargantuan creatures that emerge from the sea to terrorize unsuspecting oceanside communities seldom, if ever, wear neatly pressed tweed sports coats and gabardine slacks."

"Maybe not," agreed Sullivan, "but I thought the giant squid in its lapel was really neat. What did you think of the other movie?"

" 'The Monster That Devoured Upper Montclair, New Jersey'? A spectactular redefinition of the word 'banal'."

"Yeah, I thought it was good, too," said Sullivan, "but not *that* good."

Before Marty had a chance to respond to Sullivan's spectacular redefinition of the word 'ignorance,' his attention was diverted by Dudley's booming voice.

"This...thing...don't...work!" Dudley growled, emphasizing each word of his complaint by pounding the item in question—a shiny, metallic object—against the back of the bus stop bench.

"What is it, Dud?" asked Marty.

"A crummy pocket watch."

"Oh yeah? Let me have a look." Marty walked over to the bench and took the watch from Dudley. "Hey, this isn't a pocket watch."

"It ain't?"

"Nope. It's a stopwatch."

"Whatever it is," said Dudley, "it's busted."

"It's dented," said Marty, "but it's not broken. It works fine. Where did you get it?"

"Sportin' goods store next to the theater."

"How much was it?"

"What d'ya mean, 'How much was it?' It was free."

"Right. Of course."

"I didn't see you go into the sporting goods store, Dud," said Sullivan.

"Neither did the folks inside."

We spent the next half hour using the "free" stopwatch to time each other's dashes to the corner and back, but my participation in the impromptu track meet was, at best, half-hearted. That's because I was keeping a nervous lookout for the squad of detectives that was—I had convinced myself—assembling in a nearby parking lot at that very moment and working out a plan to take us by surprise.

"Hey, I just got a great idea," said Marty after he set yet another new world record in the bus-stop dash. "Why don't we go over to the high school and time ourselves on a real track?"

"Sounds good to me," I said, anxious for any excuse to escape the dragnet before it was too late.

"Good thinking, Mart," said Sullivan.

"Look," said Dudley, demonstrating his propensity for appropriating ideas as well as more tangible goods, "why don't we take the watch and head over to the high school?"

"Great idea, Dud," said Marty. "Why didn't I think of that?"

"Who knows?" said Dudley.

Sullivan was attempting to get to his feet when Marty first spotted her.

"Is that who I think it is?" he said, pointing toward the gate at the far end of the track.

"Yep," confirmed Sullivan, "it is indeed. What's she doing here?"

"The stopwatch!" I yelled. "The police have us surrounded and they sent her to talk us into giving ourselves up." My eyes frantically searched the roof of the school building for signs of snipers training their high-powered rifles at us.

Marty, Dudley, and Sullivan looked at me like I was crazy. "You're crazy," they chorused. They were right of course. Extreme guilt and terror used to do that to me every time.

"Besides," added Dudley, "if the cops *did* have us surrounded, she'd just tell them to shoot us."

Naturally I was embarrassed by my hysterical outburst, but my discomfort intensified enormously when it became apparent that it had attracted Sister Mary Mummy's attention.

"If it wasn't for your big mouth and your prairie nod fantasies," whispered Dudley, poking me in the chest with a rigid forefinger, "we probably coulda' hid under the stands and spied on her."

"Uh, I think you mean 'paranoid fantasies,' Dud," said Marty.

"I know what I mean," replied Dudley viciously, "an' I also know that now we're gonna have to stand around bein' polite and kissin' her a...ah, hi there, S'ter."

"Mr. Mack," nodded Sister Mary Mummy. "Boys." She was dragging a two-wheeled wire cart behind her. It was filled with grocery bags.

"Hello, S'ter."

"Say, was it my imagination, or did I hear one of you scream a few minutes ago?"

"Oh, you heard one of us scream a few minutes ago alright," said Sullivan.

"Yeah," said Dudley. "It was him."

"Stubbed my toe," I mumbled.

"I see," said Sister Mary Mummy. "That's too bad."

Unlike Dudley, I found it practically impossible to lie to a nun. Consequently, I began to babble. "Actually, S'ter, I didn't really stub my toe—not today anyhow. Of course I have stubbed it before today, many times, in fact, but..."

"So what brings you way out here, S'ter?" interjected Marty. He was trying to stop me from self-destructing right there in front of everybody.

"I was just going to ask you boys the same question."

"Well," replied Marty, "we're basically just fooling around. You know, running laps and stuff."

"Yeah, S'ter," said Sullivan. "Dudley swip...er, *found* a really neat stopwatch today. I just finished running a 4:18 880."

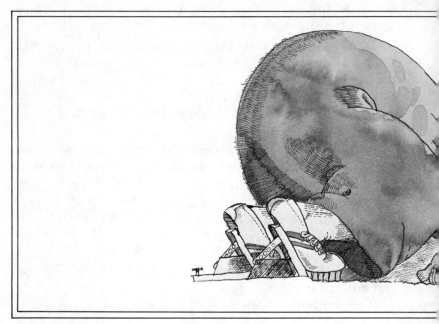

"A 4:18 *880?* How in the world did you manage to do that, Mr. Sullivan? On your hands?"

"Why didn't *I* think of that one?" muttered Dudley.

"May I take a look at the stopwatch you—what was the word Mr. Sullivan used?—ah, yes, the stopwatch you *found*?"

While she was examining the watch, Marty again gently pressed her for an explanation as to why she was at the track.

"To tell you the truth," said Sister Mary Mummy, handing the stopwatch to Dudley without comment, "I'm a little distressed that you boys have caught me here."

That was certainly a switch. We were usually distressed because she caught *us.*

"Oh yeah," said Marty casually, "how come?"

"I'll tell you if you promise never to tell anyone else. Ever."

"We promise," we promised.

"O.K. As you may or may not know, a few months ago I volunteered to do the weekly grocery shopping for the convent. It is not one of the more sought after chores in our household so I was given the assignment, along with the effusive thanks of the older Sisters and the standard request that under no circumstances was I to purchase devil's food cake mix."

"It was very generous of you to volunteer for shopping duty," said Marty.

"It would have been, Mr. Shea," replied Sister Mary Mummy, "except that I had an ulterior motive—a purely selfish ulterior motive. You see, I saw the grocery run as a chance to get out of the convent for a few hours on Saturday afternoons and to do something for myself. In other words, I saw it as a chance to spend some time here."

"Here?"

"Yes, right here on this track."

"What for?"

"Why, to run laps of course."

We were stunned. "You mean you come here every week and *run laps*?" asked Marty. "Why?"

"Simple," said Sister Mary Mummy. "Running makes me feel good and it gives me a few minutes alone to think. I tried running on the streets once, but it caused a commotion you wouldn't believe. Sister Superior really nailed my habit to the wall for that little episode. Anyway, there's never been anyone here to see me. Until today."

"How many laps do you usually run, S'ter?"

"12. Sometimes 15. It depends."

"Times?"

"Around 14 minutes for three miles; 25 minutes for five."

Marty whistled through his teeth. "Have you ever been timed in the mile?"

"No."

"Would you like to be?"

Sister Mary Mummy thought it over for a moment. "Why not?" she said. "It might be fun to run against the clock at least once before I hang up my spikes for good."

"Terrific!" shouted Marty. He reached into one of Sister Mary Mummy's overflowing grocery bags and withdrew a rolled-up cash register receipt. "Here's our official finish tape. Since Sullivan's wiped out, he can be the official timer, and we'll be your official pacers."

While Sister Mary Mummy was changing into a pair of well-worn red and white, low slung spikes, Marty conducted a pre-run briefing.

"Since it's obvious that none of us can do a mile in less than three days, I think we should take turns pacing her."

"How do we do that?" asked Dudley.

"Easy," said Marty. "Just go out and run your rear end off for 440 yards."

"But there's only three of us," I pointed out, "and a

mile is four laps."

"I know," said Marty. "You take the second lap, Dudley'll take the third, and I'll run the first and fourth."

Having received our assignments, Dudley and I joined Sullivan at the starting line. Marty and Sister Mary Mummy, meanwhile, took their positions on the track.

"On your mark, get set, GO!" yelled the official timer a few seconds later, and the runners were off.

Marty immediately cut to the inside lane and the nun quickly fell in behind him. Though Marty, by far the fastest runner at Our Lady of the Gulag, was really pouring it on, Sister Mary Mummy effortlessly matched him stride for stride during lap number one.

"Time?" shouted Marty when he crossed the line and pulled off the track at the end of the first quarter. I was already into the first turn of my pace lap, acutely aware of Sister Mary Mummy's deep, even breathing directly behind me.

"One minute, four seconds even," I heard Sullivan yell.

I was putting every ounce of energy I possessed into my sprint around the track, so it was more than a little disconcerting to hear Sister Mary Mummy say, "This is supposed to be a mile *run*, Mr. Hoffman, not a leisurely stroll. Can you please step it up a little?" I tried, but to no avail.

"Two minutes, 16 seconds," yelled Sullivan as I ran off the track and collapsed onto the infield. When I looked up, I saw that Dudley was already more than half a lap ahead of Sister Mary Mummy.

"I sent him on his way a while ago," said Marty in answer to my wordless question. "She's too strong for any of us to pace her, but he didn't want to be left out."

We watched silently as Sister Mary Mummy rapidly gained on Dudley and finally overtook him in the last few yards of the backstretch. "She's on her own now," Marty said softly.

"Three minutes, 10 seconds!" Sullivan called out when she thundered across the line and headed into her fourth and final lap.

"I don't believe it," said Marty. "She did the third quarter in 54 seconds!"

"She ain't runnin'," gasped Dudley, lumbering up to us, "she's flyin' low."

Dudley's observation was an exaggeration, to be sure, but not by much. Sister Mary Mummy *was* flying around the track. The veil of her habit was stiffly horizontal to the ground, almost as if it had been starched into that position, and her stride was long and graceful.

"If she keeps this pace up," said Marty, "she'll be pretty close to four minutes. Quick, get that tape stretched across the finish line."

While Dudley and I were unfurling the long grocery receipt I reflected on the fact that only a few years earlier Roger Bannister had become an international hero when he was the first to break the elusive, magical four-minute barrier for the mile. It had been done many times by many people since that rainy, windy Oxford day in May 1954 when the 25-year-old medical student stunned the world with a 3:59.4, but it had never been accomplished by a middle-aged nun in full religious garb on a dusty, slippery track. It occurred to me that I was witnessing history in the making.

Moments later, Sister Mary Mummy emerged from the final turn and burst into the home stretch. We had been under the impression that she had been running flat-out since the end of the second lap, but she proved us wrong when she suddenly accelerated 50 yards from the tape. The pain and agony caused by her finishing kick was etched into her features; the only sound on the track was her heavy, rhythmic breathing and the crunch of her spikes on the cinders.

"C'mon, Sister," Dudley whispered from the other end of the grocery receipt we were holding chest-high across the track, "you can do it."

As the flying nun raised her arms and lunged forward, breaking the tape, Sullivan hit the watch stem with his thumb, stopping the march of time. With Marty hanging on his shoulder, he consulted the instrument.

"3:59.9!" he shrieked. "3:59.9!"

We sprinted up the track to where Sister Mary Mummy had stopped. She was bent over at the waist with her hands on her knees, struggling to catch her breath.

"You did it, Sister," yelled Marty. "You broke four minutes."

"Let's not be too hasty," replied the out-of-breath nun. "The time means nothing; it's only an approximation."

"But…"

"I appreciate your excitement and I admit that I didn't do too badly. But while putting my performance into minutes and seconds—not to mention tenths of seconds—is interesting, it is also irrelevant."

"But…"

"This old track hasn't been measured in at least 30 years, and it may not have been laid out all that accurately to begin with."

"But…"

"And the timing device that was used is, to put it mildly, suspect. An inexpensive, badly dented stopwatch could be off considerably. In view of all that, I think it's best that we just say I ran four laps around a high school track in a fairly respectable time and leave it at that."

"But…"

"I want to thank you boys for helping me out this afternoon," said Sister Mary Mummy, depositing her track shoes into her big black purse, "and I want to thank you in advance for keeping our little secret safe."

And with that, the greatest miler ever to don a habit grabbed the handle of her grocery cart and headed for home.   ᴥ

XVIII

...THE LAST DAY

T WAS ONE OF THOSE MORNINGS when everything is exactly right with the world; you know, one of those rare and wonderful times that seem to promise the fulfillment of dreams long held and the disappearance of troubles large and small. The sun was shining (natch) and the birds were singing (ditto), but the real kicker—the icing on the ol' cake, so to speak—was simply this: the blessed and glorious event known as summer vacation was now just a few short hours away. I could hardly believe I had successfully survived nine solid months of the psychological terror so casually and expertly inflicted by Sister Mary Mummy, but it was true. A few more sweeps of the classroom clock, that bland timepiece I had come to loathe, and I would be forever free of her and of this place. My long-running nightmare was drawing to a close.

Consequently I was feeling happier and more content than I'd felt in about as long as I could remember when I strolled onto Our Lady of the Gulag's playground for the last time. And although I wasn't particularly anxious to socialize with anyone and run the risk of breaking my euphoric spell, I nevertheless headed directly toward the basketball court. Force of habit, I suppose.

As usual, Marty Shea was already occupying the dilapidated wooden bench adjacent to the court and, as usual, he had his face buried in a book that wouldn't ever be found on any eighth-grade reading list unless there's a Marquis de Sade Elementary School out there somewhere. I dropped my own load of more sedate volumes onto the bench and sat down.

"Howdy," said Marty without looking up.

"Howdy yourself," I replied for about the millionth time since we'd begun meeting like this in the first grade.

Marty slowly turned a page. He still hadn't so much as glanced at me. "So ... what's happening?" he asked, faithfully adhering to our traditional morning exchange.

"Nothing much on this end. You?" I, too, kept to the unwritten script. Tradition does, as they say, die hard.

"SOS," he yawned. "Same ol' s...*Hey, watch it!*"

A paper bag bearing several large grease stains apparently caused by the leakage of its contents had skidded across the pages of Marty's book and come to rest in his lap. Wrinkling his nose in disgust, Marty gingerly picked up the bag and held it at arm's length.

"C'mon, Mart, give it here," shrieked Jimmy Sullivan. "That's my lunch. Gimme my lunch. Please, Mart, have a heart. It's mine. *Please.*"

"Sorry, man," said Dudley Mack, lumbering up to the bench. "I didn't mean to hit you with that bag of putrid garbage. It just kinda got away from me."

"It's not a bag of garbage," screamed Sullivan, "it's my lunch!"

Nobody paid the slightest bit of attention to Sullivan. As I indicated earlier, tradition dies hard.

"That's OK," said Marty, tossing the bag to Dudley. "It

just caught me by surprise."

Dudley caught the bag, spun away from us, feinted to his right and threw an elbow into Sullivan's scrawny chest. He then put up a 15-foot jumper with the little twerp's lunch.

"Exactly how many of Sullivan's midday meals would you say Dudley has ruined?" Marty asked absently as we watched Sullivan unsuccessfully scramble for the rebound.

"Oh, I don't know. How many days have we been going to school here?"

"Let's see," said Marty. "Figure 20 days a month for nine months. That's 180 days a year times eight years, which is... which is... uh... 1440 days. Now if we subtract, say 40 days for holidays and illness, that gives us a grand total of 1400 mashed, mangled and otherwise maliciously manhandled and mutilated lunches. Give or take a few."

"Geez, you'd think Sullivan would've wised up somewhere along the line and started buying his lunch in the cafeteria."

"Hey, give the little creep some credit. He's dumb alright, but he's not *that* dumb."

"Yeah, I guess you're right."

We sat in silence for a few minutes before Marty suddenly jumped up and commenced a series of strenuous exercises. He claimed they prevented classroom fatigue. "Care to join me?" he puffed.

"No way. I'll just sit here and try to convince myself that you aren't as dumb as Sullivan." Marty had talked me into the exercises once a long time ago; I was fatigued in the classroom and everywhere else for three days afterward.

"So you're feeling pretty good, huh?" said Our Lady of the Gulag's answer to Jack LaLanne.

"Does it show?"

"Like a neon sign on a black velvet background."

"Well yeah," I admitted, "I feel terrific as a matter of fact. Just plain terrific, you know?"

"Of course I know," replied Marty incredulously. "I feel that way every day."

"I just can't believe we're finally getting ourselves out of this dump," I said, "and away from you-know-who."

"Amen to that," grunted Marty.

"Do you really feel as good as this every day?"

"I do indeed. Every day."

"Incredible," I mumbled. Then: "You know, I even found myself not disliking Sullivan a few minutes ago. I mean I actually felt sorry for him."

Marty halted his routine and stared at me. "Wow," he said, "I've never felt *that* good."

I leaned back on the bench and closed my eyes. "I can't get used to the idea that everything's so perfect; that absolutely nothing can go wrong and that..."

"Uh oh," interrupted Marty. "Something's wrong."

"Cut it out, Shea. I'm not kidding."

"Neither am I," he said. "Look over there."

I opened my eyes and looked in the direction he was pointing. A sizeable and obviously excited crowd had gathered near the jungle gym on the far side of the playground.

"A fight?"

"Can't tell from here. Probably either that or somebody fell and busted his head open." Marty picked up his books. "Let's check it out."

As we approached the milling mob we could hear shouts and sobbing, but were unable to see who was doing either.

"Excuse me, please," Marty kept repeating as he shoved his way through the underclassmen who were surrounding the action. I followed closely behind him.

A few moments later we found ourselves face-to-face with the cause of the commotion. The shouter was Mary Margaret Delicate; the sobber was Suzy Fondell. This was a switch. Normally it was the other way around.

"Terrific," muttered Marty, "the Bobbsey Twins are at it again." He was of course referring to the fact that Mary Margaret and Suzy were about as compatible as gasoline fumes and a flamethrower.

"I can't go on any longer," Suzy wailed pathetically. "My life has no meaning. No meaning at all."

"Shut up, you silly little twit," shouted Mary Margaret. "Your life's *never* had any meaning."

Hearing this, Suzy wailed even louder. There's absolutely no doubt in my mind that most of the folks within six square blocks of Our Lady of the Gulag were heading for their cellars clutching portable radios, convinced that an air raid alert had just been sounded.

"What seems to be the problem, Mary Margaret?" asked Marty.

"There's no real problem," she replied. "Little Miss Crybaby here is just a tiny bit upset and I'm trying to comfort her."

"And a darn fine job you seem to be doing, too," said Marty, whose mastery of sarcasm was surpassed only by that of Sister Mary Mummy. It was common knowledge that the good Sister held a black belt in the art.

Momentarily abandoning the object of her peculiar brand of compassion, Mary Margaret angrily confronted Marty.

"What do you mean by *that* remark?" she spat out.

"Nothing," Marty replied, "nothing at all. I was merely commenting on your, ah, somewhat unusual technique of dispensing comfort." He indicated the sobbing Suzy with a nod of his head. "However I'm afraid the jury's still out regarding its effectiveness."

Mary Margaret tried to say something, but before her enraged sputterings could transform themselves into worlds and sentences Marty promptly defused her tantrum.

"By the way," he said, "I like your outfit."

"Really?" she cooed.

"Really. It's quite a departure from your usual attire, but a fetching one, to be sure."

According to an ancient custom whose origins are lost in the mists of time, Our Lady of the Gulag's graduating—that is, eighth-grade—students were generously allowed to shed their required uniforms and wear clothing of their own choosing on the last day of school. Though in retrospect this gesture was a small, almost insignificant reward for enduring years of strictly-enforced uniformity, at the time we viewed it as a highly symbolic event heralding the freedom that was finally within easy reach.

In any event, most of us responded to the lifting of the clothing restriction in one of two ways. The vast majority, myself included, proudly dressed in a manner intended to enhance our personal appearances. Of course it didn't work for everyone, myself included, but that was the sincere aim of those of us who chose this response. The small but substantial minority, meanwhile, selected from their civilian wardrobes those items of apparel thought to have the best chance of deeply offending the faculty, who, it hardly need be pointed out, wore *their* uniforms religiously.

And then there was Mary Margaret Delicate. The outfit of which she was so obviously proud, the very same get-up for which Marty Shea had just expressed such false admiration, was an almost exact duplicate of the uniform that was so detested by each and every one of Mary Margaret's female schoolmates. It would have been a completely exact duplicate except for one thing: the embroidered "G" was missing.

"Yep," said Marty, "you look real sharp. But tell me, don't you feel just a little bit *naked* without your 'G'?"

His emphasis on the word naked caused Mary Margaret to blanch. "*Sin!*" she screeched, backing away and pointing at Marty. "That's a sin, a big one." She slammed her hands over her ears and shut her eyes. "A sin. I heard a sin and it's not even 8:30 in the morning." Mary Margaret turned her back and began to moan softly. It never did take much to send her off the deep end.

Needless to say, my euphoria was rapidly slipping away. In fact, I was practically feeling like my old self as I stood there surrounded by the murmuring crowd, watching Suzy Fondell crying her eyes out and listening to Mary Margaret Delicate praying for deliverance. I didn't even notice that Dudley Mack had arrived and was standing right behind me.

Suddenly Mary Margaret spun around and faced us. "Get out of here," she yelled. "I never want to see you again, you lousy, rotten *sinner!*"

Though her request was directed at Marty, it was Dudley who spoke.

"I ain't goin' no place," he said, "an' I ain't a lousy, rotten sinner. I'm pretty good at it, even if I do say so myself."

"What's going on, guys?" said Sullivan from somewhere on the outer fringes of the crowd.

"Yeah," said Dudley, "what's all this about?"

"Nothing," replied Marty. "I merely asked Mary Margaret if she felt naked. Apparently either the word or the concept offended her."

"Naked?" said Dudley. "She's doin' all this carrying' on about sayin' 'naked'?"

"Yep."

"Why hell, M.M.," Dudley said, "naked ain't *nothin'*. Now if you wanna hear somethin' bad, try this..."

Whatever epithet Dudley chose from his impressive repertoire lost in Mary Margaret's equally impressive scream.

"*Noooooooooooooooooo!*"

Then she was gone, taking her scream with her. It certainly wasn't the first time we had watched her leave the playground in tears and sprint toward the sanctuary of the school building, but I devoutly hoped it would be the last.

When Mary Margaret was out of sight, Dudley addressed the crowd. "OK, the show's over. Let's move on." It usually takes several minutes to disperse a large group, but this one scattered immediately. Undoubtedly the fact that Dudley was casually displaying an open switchblade had some bearing on the efficiency with which his command was obeyed.

When the evacuation was complete, only Dudley, Marty, Suzy, Sullivan and myself remained in the area of the jungle gym.

"Uh, can I stay, Dud?" asked Sullivan.

Dudley appeared to be on the verge of telling Sullivan to get lost, but something made him change his mind. Perhaps he had suddenly remebered that Sullivan's family was moving to New Jersey the following day and he realized his favorite target for harassment wouldn't be available much longer.

"Your family really movin' to New York tomorrow?" asked Dudley.

"New *Jersey*," whined Sullivan. "Yes, it's really true."

"An' they're still plannin' to take you with them?"

"Of course they are."

"You sure about that? I mean, maybe they're packin' up an' leavin' right this minute. Maybe they was just lettin' you *think* they was gonna take you along so you wouldn't cause a big stink or somethin'."

"No, they're taking me with them alright," said Sullivan confidently, "and we're leaving tomorrow at 10:00. I saw the plane tickets and one of them had my name on it."

"Well," drawled Dudley, "I still think it's a trick. Yeah, you can stay, but keep your mouth shut or I'll punch out your lights."

"Right, Dud," said Sullivan happily.

Dudley then turned his attention to Suzy Fondell. The

rest of us were too taken aback by her mysterious (to us) emotional outburst to do anything but stand there and dumbly stare at her. Dudley, however, walked right up to where she was leaning against the rusty jungle gym. He bent down and began to gather up her books that lay scattered on the lumpy asphalt.

"Are you thinking what I'm thinking?" mumbled Marty as we watched this tender scene.

"Beauty and the beast?"

"Right."

And it was true. Dudley, the hulking throwback to Neanderthal times, looked even more uncivilized than usual in his battered motorcycle boots, oil-spattered, torn jeans, and a baggy sweatshirt that appeared to have been laundered using a seven-course meal for detergent. Suzy, on the other hand, was a vision of loveliness in her bright pink skirt and sweater. A matching pink ribbon gathered her long, blonde hair into a luxurious ponytail. Like the rest of us, Dudley was hopelessly infatuated with Suzy's physical beauty; unlike the rest of us, he was also captivated by her alleged mind which was one attribute she kept well hidden, if indeed it existed at all.

"Don't let ol' M.M. get to you," Dudley said to Suzy, handing over her books. "She just plain ain't worth gettin' yourself all worked up over."

"Mary Margaret isn't the reason I'm standing here blubbering," said Suzy softly. "It's my parents."

"Your parents?" said Dudley. "You mean your mom and your dad?"

"Yes."

"So you're upset because of your mom and dad, your parents?"

"Oh, no," cried Suzy, "I'm not upset *because* of my parents; I'm upset because of what my parents *did* to me."

"Your mom and dad?"

"Yes."

"Lord," muttered Marty under his breath, "this could

take all day."

"Well at least we know that she's upset and that she has parents," I whispered.

"What did your parents do to you?" asked Dudley.

Suzy looked away and I could see that her chin was quivering and that a giant tear was forming in her right eye. Dudley had obviously struck a nerve.

"It's terrible," she finally said, fighting to maintain her composure. "They...told me last night that I have to go to Sacred Heart next year."

Dudley was shocked, stunned. "That *is* terrible," he said. "Would you excuse me for a moment?" Suzy, caught up in another attack of sobbing, nodded her head.

Dudley approached us with a grave look on his face.

"She has to go to Sacred Heart next year," he whispered, "and that's terrible.

"We heard," said Marty.

"Listen," said Dudley, leaning close to Marty's ear, "*why* is that terrible?"

"Beats me, Dud. Why don't you ask her?"

Dudley ambled back over to Suzy.

"Sacred Heart, huh?"

"Yes."

"I always thought that was a pretty good school. I mean they have all these nice lookin' chicks over there, an'..."

"That's just the point," interrupted Suzy, "Sacred Heart's a *girls'* school."

"So?"

"So there's no boys there, which means there's no football team, which means they don't have *cheerleaders*. I was planning to major in cheerleading, but my parents absolutely refuse to let me go to Dick Clark High like I wanted to." She sighed heavily. "Now it looks like the only event I'll get to cheer at is the annual Sacred Heart bake sale."

"Excuse me, Suzy," said Marty," but I couldn't help

overhearing. Actually, Sacred Heart does have a cheer-leading squad."

"It does?"

"Yep. Of course they don't cheer for Sacred Heart's athletic teams because as you've so astutely pointed out, Sacred Heart has no athletic teams. They do, however, lend loud and lusty support to the Bulldogs of good ol' St. Timothy High."

"The boys' school on the other side of town?"

"The very same."

Suzy's veil of despair was lifting. "What are their uniforms like?"

"I don't know...maroon jerseys, white pants, and maroon helmets with a bulldog on the side," replied Marty.

"Helmets?" shouted Suzy. "I can't wear a helmet. Nobody'll be able to see my hair."

"Oh, you mean the *cheerleaders'* uniforms," said Marty. "I guess they're basically your standard rah rah duds in maroon and white."

"Maroon's only my eighth favorite color," said Suzy, "but I suppose a maroon uniform is better than no uniform."

"That's one way of looking at it."

"Well, maybe Sacred Heart won't be so bad after all," said Suzy.

"Of course it won't," said Marty. "Besides, we'll probably be seeing each other on the sidelines next fall."

"Oh, are you going to be a Sacred Heart cheerleader, too?"

"Not exactly," Marty replied patiently. "But I *am* going to try out for St. Tim's football team." Suzy looked very confused, a not unusual occurrence with her. "You know," said Marty, "the boys' school whose teams you'll be rooting for?"

"Oh, right," giggled Suzy. "I forgot." She looked over at me and smiled. "Are you going to St. Tom's, too?"

"St. Tim's," I said. "No, I'm not. I am going to abandon

Mr. Shea here to the iron-fisted Jesuits who, it is said, make our beloved Sister Mary Mummy look like Rebecca of Sunnybrook Farm, while I pursue the next phase of my education in the far more relaxed atmosphere of Jimmy Piersall High School."

"What about you, Dudley?"

"I hadn't thought about it much," he answered. "I sorta figured this was the end of school for me before I found out about this stupid law that says you gotta keep goin' 'til you're 16. Anyway, I s'pose I'll go to Piersall until I'm 16."

"I'm going to attend an exclusive prep school in New Jersey," announced Sullivan, "but I doubt if any of you care about that."

"It's taken eight years," said Marty incredulously, "but he's finally starting to catch on."

At that moment the bell summoning us to class rang.

⌖

Sister Mary Mummy appeared to be in very high spirits as we filed past her into the classroom. The stern, almost ferocious manner she normally displayed during this grim daily ceremony had been replaced by a mood that could be described as approaching jovial. This was more than a little surprising because we had fully expected her to seize every opportunity on this last day of school to get in some final licks. It could still happen of course, but our first half-minute or so in her presence had passed uneventfully.

Even Dudley Mack and Suzy Fondell, two individuals who possessed the unenviable ability to arouse Sister Mary Mummy's ire just by showing up, had received only a smiling "Good morning."

"Can you believe it?" whispered Marty Shea. "She didn't frisk Dudley and she didn't hand Suzy a Kleenex and tell her to wipe off her lip gloss."

"Maybe she's finally mellowing."

"Right. And maybe Monsignor Munchkin's the Tooth

Fairy."

Gradually the room became quiet enough to hear a pin drop, which was exactly the way Sister Mary Mummy liked it. Before she had a chance to speak, however, the silence was shattered by a metallic sound.

"Sorry, S'ter," mumbled Tina Azzaro from her seat in the back row, "I dropped a pin."

"I see," smiled Sister Mary Mummy. Then, taking up her usual position in front of her desk, she addressed the class. "I bet most of you never thought this day would arrive, did you?"

"No, S'ter."

"And I'll further wager," she continued, "that most of you think I have something truly diabolical prepared for you today, right?"

"Yes, S'ter," we laughed nervously.

"I thought so," she said. "Unfortunately, I'm afraid I'll have to disappoint you. I stayed up half the night trying to come up with something spectacular, something to send you off in grand style, but I couldn't think of a single thing."

Of course no one in the room believed her. Not for one minute.

"As a result of my inability to concoct a new and exotic form of mass torture," said Sister Mary Mummy with a sly wink, "our sole activity today will consist of turning in the textbooks Our Lady of the Gulag has lent you this year with such generosity and, I might add, with such faith. When that distasteful, but necessary task is accomplished, you will be dismissed until 3:00 this afternoon when you and your guests will assemble in the cafeteria to participate in the graduation ceremonies."

This announcement was greeted with cheers and loud applause. Sister Mary Mummy wasn't such a bad guy after all, I thought to myself. The object of my sudden affection abruptly halted the impromptu demonstration by raising her arms.

"Now, before we get on with the business of turning in our texts, I have a few things I'd like to say."

"Watch out," murmured Marty, "here it comes. I knew she was just setting us up for the kill."

"First of all," said Sister Mary Mummy, "I wish to compliment you on your appearances. Generally speaking, you present a very pleasing sight. This may surprise you, but I'm not especially fond of the drab uniforms our students are required to wear. It can become very boring staring at people who wear the same thing every day." She then pointed to her habit and said, "But of course you already know that."

This line drew more applause and whistles of appreciation.

"I am especially relieved to see that Miss Fondell made it safely to class without being ambushed by a pack of nearsighted flamingo poachers. Unfortunately, Mr. Mack seems to have fared less well on his morning journey. Tell me, Mr. Mack, was anyone seriously injured?"

"Whatd'ya mean, S'ter?"

"Was anyone hurt in the accident?"

"What accident?"

"The one that damaged your apparel so severely."

The class was really howling now, all except Suzy Fondell, that is. She was trying to look up 'flamingo' in her dictionary.

"I wasn't in no accident," said Dudley when the laughter subsided.

"I wasn't in *an* acci..." Sister Mary Mummy stopped herself and smiled. "Oops, I almost fell into *that* trap again; I almost said, 'I wasn't in *an* accident.' Naturally, Mr. Mack would then innocently pretend that my attempt to correct his grammar was actually a statement of fact and he'd say something like, 'That's great, S'ter, we both wasn't in no accident.' Well, Mr. Mack, let me try another approach. In attempting to say that you weren't involved in an accident, you used a double negative. In effect you actually said you *were* in an accident."

"No I didn't, S'ter," protested Dudley. "I said, 'I wasn't in no accident' because I really wasn't in no accident. Honest."

"An accident," thundered a thoroughly exasperated Sister Mary Mummy. "I wasn't in *an* accident."

"Me neither." The truly amazing thing about this rather bizarre exchange was that Dudley wasn't pretending. His lack of understanding was absolutely genuine.

Sister Mary Mummy stared at Dudley and slowly shook her head. After several minutes, she spoke again.

"Mr. Mack," she said, "do you know what a vow is?"

"Of course I do, S'ter. Do you think I'm some kinda dummy or somethin'?"

"We won't go into that now," she replied. "I just wanted to make sure you know what a vow is."

"How come?" asked Dudley.

"Because you're going to see me break one of mine. Oh, not one of the sacred vows I took when I became a nun, but a personal vow I made to myself when I began my teaching career. When I received my first teaching assignment several hundred years ago, I promised myself that I would never, under any circumstances, allow myself to be defeated in a battle of wits with a student. I kept that solemn promise for a long, long time, Mr. Mack, but now I am forced to break it. I am forced to say that you win. I hereby concede." Sister Mary Mummy paused for a minute before adding, "For the time being, anyway."

We weren't quite sure what she meant by that, but it sounded pretty ominous. Even Dudley seemed worried.

"Oh, I almost forgot," continued Sister Mary Mummy, "there's one more piece of business to get out of the way. Shortly before the morning bell rang, I was informed that Mr. Shea and Mr. Mack were roaming the playground spewing swear words. Would these two gentlemen please stand and tell me whether or not the charge has any validity."

While Marty and Dudley got out of their chairs I sneaked a look at Mary Margaret Delicate, the stool pigeon. She was clearly enjoying this scene.

"As long as you're on your feet, Mr. Mack," said Sister Mary Mummy, "why don't you just stroll on up here and give me your knife?"

Dudley shuffled to the front of the room and handed it over.

"Where did you get this one?" asked Sister Mary Mummy.

"My mother gave it to me," replied Dudley. "For my birthday."

"How thoughtful of her," said Sister Mary Mummy. She opened a desk drawer and dropped the switchblade inside. "Thanks to you Mr. Mack, I do believe I am now the proud possessor of the Western Hemisphere's largest private cutlery collection. Now, Mr. Shea, why don't you either confirm or deny the charge against you."

"OK, S'ter," said Marty. "I plead guilty as charged."

Sister Mary Mummy was obviously surprised by Marty's prompt admission of guilt, especially since he didn't claim there were extenuating circumstances involved.

"You mean you admit you spewed obscenities?"

"Actually, I only spewed one."

"I see."

"I spewed the word 'naked.' "

"Naked?" repeated Sister Mary Mummy, casting a stony glance in Mary Margaret's direction.

"Yes, S'ter. Naked."

"And you, Mr. Mack? Are you guilty as well?"

"No way, S'ter. I didn't say nuthin'. I just pretended I was gonna say somethin' real terrible cuz' ol' Mary Mudface was actin' all hysterical about hearin' Marty say 'naked'. Anyway, I made like I was about to really lay one on her, but she let out this scream that could be heard from hell to breakfast and then headed for the hills."

"Case dismissed," said Sister Mary Mummy. "Thank you, Mr. Shea, Mr. Mack. You may sit down."

Marty and Dudley, grinning broadly, resumed their seats but not before each had given Mary Margaret a friendly wave. Mary Margaret looked very ill.

It was a little after 11 when we finished turning in our borrowed books and were once again called to order by Sister Mary Mummy.

"I suppose I could give you a little speech about how wonderful it was having all of you in my class this past year," she said, "but I think I'll save my official farewell address for the graduation ceremony. I would like Miss Fondell, Miss Azzaro, Mr. Mack, Mr. Littlefield, and Mr. Goldberg to remain behind for a few minutes. The rest of you are excused until 3:00 p.m. this afternoon."

While the rest of the class stampeded toward the door, I joined Marty and Sullivan at Dudley's desk.

"We'll be waiting for you at the park, Dud. In the usual spot."

"Gotcha," smiled Dudley wanly.

&

"What do you think happened to him?" asked Sullivan for the dozenth time in the past 15 minutes. We had been hanging around the park a few blocks from Our Lady of the Gulag for over three hours and Dudley still hadn't shown.

"I don't know," muttered Marty, "but something's definitely wrong."

"Hey," shouted Sullivan, "here he comes."

Sure enough, the familiar figure of Dudley Mack was slowly trudging up the hill toward us.

"He doesn't look too chipper, does he?"

"No," I replied. "He looks like an 80-year-old wino."

A few minutes later we discovered that Dudley felt as bad as he looked. We also discovered why.

"She ain't gonna promote me outta that place," he

said.

"*What?*"

"You heard me," said Dudley. "I gotta go back to the good ol' Gulag again next year."

"To her class?"

"You got it, buddy. She said my academic progress wasn't sufficient to justify advancement to the next level or some such b.s."

"What about the others? Fondell, Azzaro, Littlefield and Goldberg?"

"She shafted them, too."

"Geez, that's really tough," said Marty, "Is Suzy upset?"

"Naw, not really. At least she wasn't too freaked out until S'ter told her she couldn't be a cheerleader next year until her grades got a whole lot better. That's when Suzy said she was gonna go home and strangle herself with one of those puff balls she's always shakin'." Dudley didn't say anything for a few minutes, and neither did we. "Ah, hell," he finally muttered, "I guess it won't be so bad spendin' another year there as long as ol' Suzy's around, *if* she don't strangle herself, that is."

"Yeah, I guess not," said Marty.

"Anyway, I just stopped by here to let you guys know what happened before you heard it from somebody on the street or somethin'. And since I ain't goin' to be at the graduation, I figured I better say so long to Sullivan here. So long, Sullivan."

"So long, Dud." said a choked up Sullivan. "You've been a good friend."

"No I haven't," said Dudley. "You just think so because you've never had a real friend." He began to walk back down the hill. "I guess I'll be seein' you guys around."

"Right," said Marty.

"Right," I said.

"I'd write you some letters from New Jersey," said Sul-

livan, "but I know you aren't too good at reading. How
about if I send you some pictures?"

"Buzz off, Sullivan," shouted Dudley Mack. He didn't
stop walking, and he didn't turn around.

~

Still deeply shaken by the enormity of Dudley's misfortune, I sat through the graduation ceremony in Our
Lady of the Gulag's dingy cafeteria without paying much
attention to the proceedings. I knew full well that Dudley
was a prime candidate for being held back, but I figured
the chances of it actually happening were fairly slim. I
had discussed it with Marty a few weeks earlier and he,
too, agreed that Sister Mary Mummy would most likely
pass him simply to get rid of him. After all, that's what
each of Dudley's other teachers had done.

Because I was preoccupied I only heard a few snatches
of Monsignor Munchkin's speech to the graduates and
the proud parents who had assembled to witness the
great event, but I figured I didn't miss a whole lot. I didn't
listen to a single word of Mary Margaret Delicate's vale-
dictory address and I *know* I didn't miss a thing. I did,
however, pay close attention to Sister Mary Mummy's
brief remarks. I even memorized them.

"I've enjoyed having each and every one of you as a
student these past few months," she said in a monotone.
"Good luck to you all."

That was it. Finito. No sharp sarcasm, no insightful
advice, no snappy one-liners, no nothing. Just one more
letdown in a day filled with them.

Then we were called (alphabetically, of course) to the
makeshift stage to pick up our diplomas, an exercise that
required shaking hands with both Monsignor Munchkin
and Sister Mary Mummy. Clutching my diploma as I
made my way back to my assigned seat, I felt a thick veil
of loneliness and despair envelope me. I could hardly
believe that just a few hours earlier I had felt like I was on
top of the world.

"Oh well," I said to myself, "at least it can't get any worse."

Yep, that's what I said to myself alright, and despite a long history of truly spectacular miscalculations, I had never been more wrong. It did get worse, much worse, and quickly, too.

Even now, some two decades later, I cannot think about what transpired over the next few minutes without breaking into a cold sweat. Though it will undoubtedly work a tremendous emotional hardship on me to relate the particulars here, I shall nevertheless do so. I'm just that kind of selfless person.

Anyway, here goes:

I had returned to my seat—a beige metal folding chair, as I recall—after picking up my diploma, which was encased in a smart, green folder, and I had promptly drifted off on a wave of self-pity such as I'd never experienced before. I was just being carried along, not putting up much of a fight at all, when I suddenly felt something sharp jabbing me in the ribs. Eventually, I realized the sharp thing was Howard Hall's elbow.

"Wha?"

"You won," Howard shouted, "you won!" At least that's what it sounded like he was saying.

"Huh? Wha?" It seemed like everyone in the cafeteria was on their feet, applauding and yelling.

"Wha?"

"The scholarship, man! You won the scholarship!"

All of a sudden I was hit by the proverbial ton of bricks everyone's always talking about. Hit, nothing; I was *flattened!*

The scholarship Howard Hall was yelling about was one of Our Lady of the Gulag's two, and therefore quite prestigious, annual awards. It was a four-year, full-ride to St. Timothy's—expensive St. Timothy's—that was presented to Our Lady of the Gulag's most outstanding male graduate each year. (The outstanding female graduate received a similar scholarship to Sacred Heart.) A committee consisting of Sister Superior, Monsignor Munchkin and Sister Mary Mummy chose the recipients of these awards.

I grabbed Howard Hall's arm and yanked him down to my level. "I couldn't have won," I hissed into his ear, "Shea won."

"No, he didn't. You did."

"No," I shouted. "Shea did. He even wrote an acceptance speech."

"Yeah, I thought he'd get it, and so did everybody else, but Monsignor just announced *your* name."

"Don't just sit there, son," called Monsignor Munchkin from the podium. "C'mon up here and say a few words of gratitude."

Somehow I managed to stand up on my rubbery legs. Everything was pretty blurry now, but out of the corner of my eye I caught a glimpse of my parents. From the expressions of pride on their faces I knew there was no way I was going to talk them into letting me turn down the scholarship. That's right, I wanted nothing more than to refuse the honor that had been bestowed upon me. I'd heard enough stories about the Jesuits who taught at St. Timothy's to know I wanted no part of *that* action. It looked like I was going to get it though. I was trapped and there was no way out.

But how did it happen? How did I end up in this mess? I mean, there was no way I could have been considered the most outstanding male graduate of my class. Pretty good, yes; most outstanding, no way. Sure, I always got decent grades, but only because I was afraid not to, and yes, I mostly kept my mouth shut and mostly stayed out of trouble. I was also only a fair athlete. "Versatile" is how the coaches always described me. That meant: "He probably won't do a whole lot of good, but then again he probably won't screw up too badly." But Marty Shea got better grades, Dudley Mack was a better athlete, Dave "Fat"

Chance kept his mouth shut completely and Howard Hall never got into any trouble at all. These thoughts were running through my mind when it suddenly occurred to me why I'd won. Of course! It was so simple, so obvious. I had won the lousy scholarship not because I was the best at anything; I had won merely because I was adequate in so many different areas. I was, in other words, the best of a bad lot.

In the middle of my long and tortuous journey to the platform where Monsignor Munchkin and Sister Mary Mummy awaited me, I stopped to say a few words to Marty Shea. He was slumped in an aisle seat and he had his face hidden behind his hands.

"Marty," I whispered urgently, "I don't know how this happened. I wanted you to win, I swear I did. You *know* I don't want to go to St. Tim's. That's the last place in the world I want to spend four years." He ignored me. "Marty," I pleaded, "please say something."

He slowly took his hands away from his face and looked at me through red-rimmed eyes. "OK," he snarled, "I'll say something. Go pick up your crummy scholarship... *traitor!*"

Everything that happened after that is pretty hazy. Apparently I made it to the stage where I accepted my award certificate and delivered a clumsy but well-received speech of thanks, but I honestly don't remember doing either of those things. I do, however, recall the scene that erupted when Mary Margaret Delicate found out she hadn't won the Sacred Heart scholarship for being the most outstanding female graduate. Of course you either had to be in a coma or out of the state to miss one of Mary Margaret's outbursts, and I wasn't that far gone. Almost, but not quite.

At least I didn't have to be shot up with tranquilizers and carried out of the cafeteria on a stretcher. Nor did I have to spend three months in a quiet sanitarium, all of which happened to Mary Margaret. She really went out in a blaze of glory, bless her cold, twisted little heart.

I, on the other hand, internalized my desperation, and went out quietly.

Yep, Sister Mary Mummy really did a number on us that last day.

She got me good by giving me a scholarship I didn't want (there's absolutely no doubt in my mind that she alone was responsible for that foul deed);

She got Mary Margaret Delicate and Marty Shea good by not giving them the scholarships they desperately wanted;

She got Suzy Fondell good by taking away her pompons;

She got Dudley Mack good by refusing to let him go.

It was a real virtuoso performance.

Ironically, only Jimmy Sullivan, the class chancre, escaped unscathed. That fact alone proves there's no justice in the world.

And although I haven't once laid eyes on Sister Mary Mummy since that long ago afternoon, she's never been very far from my thoughts. Matter of fact, I used to think of her every time I faced the wrath of the Jesuits at St. Tim's, which was often enough to qualify as constantly.